'Lucas is not my nephew.' Her voice was quiet, but her heart was beating so loudly it almo**...** is my son.'

'What?'

Theo stared at her in **...** heard her correctly.

'Lucas is my son,' Kerry repeated.

She looked pale and sick, but she was meeting his gaze straight on—and he knew she was utterly serious. Then, almost as if his mind was working in slow motion, his thoughts pulled together to reach another obvious conclusion.

Kerry had said that Lucas was six months old. That meant…six months…plus nine months…

'He is my son.'

The words sliced through the air like a knife—like a giant blade slicing through the reality of Theo's tightly disciplined and controlled world.

He had a son.

'You will regret this.'

'Having your son?' Her voice was thin and tremulous, as if she could sense the anger that was starting to build within him after the initial shock had sunk in.

'The fact that you kept him from me,' he said.

Natalie Rivers grew up in the Sussex countryside. As a child she always loved to lose herself in a good book, or in games that gave free rein to her imagination. She went to Sheffield University, where she met her husband in the first week of term. It was love at first sight and they have been together ever since, moving to London after graduating, getting married and having two wonderful children.

After university Natalie worked in a lab at a medical research charity, and later retrained to be a primary school teacher. Now she is lucky enough to be able to combine her two favourite occupations—being a full-time mum and writing passionate romances.

THE DIAKOS
BABY SCANDAL

BY
NATALIE RIVERS

MILLS & BOON
Pure reading pleasure™

DID YOU PURCHASE THIS BOOK WITHOUT A COVER?

If you did, you should be aware it is **stolen property** as it was reported
unsold and destroyed by a retailer. Neither the author nor the publisher
has received any payment for this book.

All the characters in this book have no existence outside the imagination
of the author, and have no relation whatsoever to anyone bearing the
same name or names. They are not even distantly inspired by any
individual known or unknown to the author, and all the incidents are
pure invention.

All Rights Reserved including the right of reproduction in whole or
in part in any form. This edition is published by arrangement with
Harlequin Enterprises II BV/S.à.r.l. The text of this publication or
any part thereof may not be reproduced or transmitted in any form
or by any means, electronic or mechanical, including photocopying,
recording, storage in an information retrieval system, or otherwise,
without the written permission of the publisher.

This book is sold subject to the condition that it shall not, by way of
trade or otherwise, be lent, resold, hired out or otherwise circulated
without the prior consent of the publisher in any form of binding or
cover other than that in which it is published and without a similar
condition including this condition being imposed on the subsequent
purchaser.

® and TM are trademarks owned and used by the trademark owner
and/or its licensee. Trademarks marked with ® are registered with the
United Kingdom Patent Office and/or the Office for Harmonisation in
the Internal Market and in other countries.

First published in Great Britain 2009
Harlequin Mills & Boon Limited,
Eton House, 18-24 Paradise Road, Richmond, Surrey TW9 1SR

© Natalie Rivers 2009

ISBN: 978 0 263 87215 6

Set in Times Roman 10½ on 12¾ pt
01-0609-44958

Printed and bound in Spain
by Litografia Rosés, S.A., Barcelona

THE DIAKOS
BABY SCANDAL

CHAPTER ONE

KERRY was shaking as she looked down at the little white stick clutched in her hand—a plus sign was clearly visible in the window. The test was positive. A flutter of excitement rose up inside her—she was pregnant.

It wasn't planned, and she hadn't truly expected the test to come up positive—but she knew the discovery that she was pregnant would change her life for ever.

She pressed her teeth gently into her lower lip and stared at the test result for a moment longer. Her heart had instantly filled with joy at the prospect of having a baby—but her body had already started to tremble with nerves.

How would Theo react to the news that he was going to be a father? The thought of telling him sent a wave of apprehension rolling through her.

It was only six months since she'd become the live-in lover of Theo Diakos—one of Athens' richest, most powerful property tycoons. She'd shared his high-paced cosmopolitan lifestyle and spent night after glorious night in his bed. He'd treated her like a princess, and his close family members—his brother, Corban, and his wife, Hallie—had made her more than welcome.

But, although Kerry had fallen deeply in love with Theo, they had never discussed their feelings for each other. And they'd never talked about their future together.

She lifted her head, pushed her long blonde hair back from her face and walked out onto the roof garden. When she and Theo were staying in the city, this magical green and scented oasis was her favourite place. The warm fragrance of climbing roses wrapped around her and the gentle sound of trickling water filled the evening air. There was such an aura of tranquillity that it was hard to imagine the garden was right on top of one of the glitziest hotels in the city—the flagship property in Theo's empire.

Beneath her the city lights were starting to shine, and up high on the Acropolis Rock the floodlit columns of the Parthenon were glowing majestically against the darkening sky. It was an awe-inspiring sight, and one that would be forever linked in her mind with Theo. Being with him was wonderful. For the first time in twenty-three years she felt as if she was wanted—cherished, even.

At first she'd hardly been able to believe that he was interested in an ordinary girl like her, but the intensity of their whirlwind affair had swept her doubts away and she'd never been so happy.

The troubles that haunted her past had faded until they seemed almost to belong to another lifetime. It was wonderful, knowing that he valued her and wanted to be with her. It was something she'd never experienced before—but it was something that she was determined her baby would feel right from the start of its life.

She pressed her hand against her stomach. The knowledge that she was carrying Theo's child was still sinking in—but she knew one thing for sure. This baby would always feel wanted. Always feel loved.

Suddenly a rush of excitement bubbled through her body. Theo *would* be happy. She was certain of it. After all, he was a wonderful uncle—he clearly thought the world of his nephew, Nicco—and she knew he would be an amazing father.

All at once she was desperate to tell him the news immediately. She hurried back inside and dashed straight to Theo's study in their private apartments at the hotel, almost running in her enthusiasm. She couldn't wait to see the look on his face when she shared her wonderful secret.

She slid to a halt outside his study door as she realised he wasn't alone. He was with his brother, Corban, and from the sound of their voices they were discussing something important—something urgent. She paused to catch her breath, disappointed that her special news would have to wait.

Then, just as she turned to leave, the subject of their conversation suddenly became clear to her. She truly had not meant to eavesdrop, and her Greek was still far from perfect. But she knew enough to understand what Theo and Corban were discussing.

They were talking about taking little Nicco away from his mother.

A knot tightened in her stomach and her heart lurched horribly in her chest. She couldn't really have understood correctly. Could she? She stood frozen outside the study door—unable to tear herself away—listening to them talk.

'You *must* think about Nicco—it's your duty to protect him,' Theo said. 'He is your son, and his well-being must come first.'

'But Hallie is my wife—she trusts me,' Corban said. 'I don't think I can do this to her.'

'You must.' Theo's voice was emphatic. 'A Diakos child belongs with the Diakos family. And Hallie is not fit to take care of your son.'

'But it seems so drastic,' Corban said. 'Can't we at least let her see Nicco before we take him?'

'No. Absolutely not,' Theo said. 'This is the only way. If we do this right now—*tonight*—Nicco can be away by helicopter to the island before Hallie even notices he's gone. Then we can deal with her privately—get her out of the country without any fuss. No one outside the family ever needs to know.'

Kerry clamped her hand over her mouth in horror. Theo and his brother were plotting to take Hallie's child away from her.

She started shaking violently, suddenly revisiting all the pain and misery of her own childhood. She felt sick, remembering the heartbreak and despair—*the utter wretchedness*—of her own true mother, who had been unable to bear having her baby daughter taken from her.

Kerry could not stand by and let that happen to Hallie.

She had to try and save her friend the anguish that her mother had suffered. Maybe if her mother had been allowed to keep her baby she would still be alive today.

Suddenly Kerry found herself backing unsteadily away from the study doorway. Her throat was tight, her stomach was knotted painfully and her mind was spinning with horrible memories that made it impossible to think straight. All she knew was that she couldn't let them take Hallie's child away from her.

She turned and ran to find her friend. She had to warn her.

She charged into the luxury apartment Hallie shared with Corban, stumbled through the huge open living space to the bedroom and found Hallie sitting in front of the mirror brushing her long brown hair.

'Kerry!' Hallie exclaimed, her cheeks flushed and her dark eyes wide with surprise. 'Is everything all right?'

'I'm sorry…' Kerry gasped for breath after her mad dash. 'It's Nicco. I heard Corban and Theo talking—they are going to take Nicco away tonight.'

'Why? What's wrong? Is he all right?' Hallie demanded, standing up so quickly that the stool she'd been sitting on crashed over.

'Yes, he's fine,' Kerry said. 'But listen—you don't understand. They said you're not fit to look after him. They're going to take Nicco away by helicopter without telling you.'

'No. They can't do that.' For a moment Hallie stood glued to the spot, her face blank with shock. Then her expression changed and she lurched into action, snatching her handbag from the dressing table so quickly that she sent a glass of wine flying. 'They won't take him. I won't let them,' she said, grabbing her car keys from a side table and hurrying unsteadily across the room in high heels. 'I'll take him away with me—somewhere they won't find us.'

'Wait,' Kerry said, automatically reaching for a handful of tissues to stem the spread of the red wine across Hallie's dressing table. 'I'll come with…'

Suddenly Kerry hesitated, looking down at the wine-soaked tissues. Hallie had been drinking. Remembering her flushed cheeks, and the way she'd swayed unevenly across the room, she'd obviously had quite a lot—way too much to be driving. But she'd just taken her car keys.

Kerry burst out of the room after her. But it was too late—the nursery door was open and Nicco's cot was empty. A glance at the lights above the family's private elevator told her that someone had already reached the underground car park.

Oh, God! What had she done? Hallie was drunk and she was about to drive out into the busy city traffic with her little boy in the car.

Kerry's heart was in her mouth as she hurtled back to Theo's study. She careered through the open door, making Theo and Corban look up in surprise.

'It's Hallie!' she cried, struggling to catch her breath to speak.

Theo was beside her in an instant. His strong hands closed reassuringly on her upper arms to keep her steady and his dark brown eyes held her secure in his powerful gaze.

'Take a deep breath.' His calm, assured voice cut through the panic that gripped her. 'That's it. Now, tell me what has happened.'

Kerry stared up at his handsome face, momentarily torn between the distress she'd felt when she heard him planning to take Nicco away from his mother and the comfort she instinctively felt simply from being close to him, from the feel of his strong hands on her arms.

'Hallie has taken Nicco in her car,' she blurted. 'She's been drinking.'

Corban cursed in Greek, then ran out the door, shouting urgently to Theo as he left. At the same time Theo spun away from Kerry to pick up the phone. She realised he was calling his security team to give orders that Hallie should not be allowed to leave.

Kerry folded her arms across her chest and hugged herself tightly. What had she done? Theo and Corban had no right to take Nicco away from his mother—but her impulsive reaction had put both mother and child in danger. She should never have acted without thinking things through.

'I'm going to help my brother,' Theo said, turning to leave. 'Hallie was away from the hotel before I warned Security, but Corban is right behind her.'

Kerry bit her quivering lip anxiously and felt her eyes burning with unshed tears. She wished she'd realised sooner that Hallie had been drinking—but it had never occurred to her that her friend would be in that state.

'It will be all right.' Suddenly Theo was back by her side, pulling her gently against his strong chest. He lifted his hands and slipped them under her hair, cradling the back of her head tenderly as he tipped her face up to his. 'You did the right thing—we'll take care of it now.'

Then, before she could reply, he was gone. But the warm, exotic fragrance of his cologne lingered in the air and the nape of her neck still tingled where his fingertips had brushed.

Theo was everything to her. Since the day she'd met him everything else in her life had faded into insignificance.

When her temporary job in Athens had finished she'd been overwhelmed with joy when he had asked her to stay with him. With his encouragement she had delayed looking for a new position, so that she would be free to travel with him wherever he went. He'd said that he wanted her with him always, so that they would be able to spend time together whenever his demanding schedule allowed.

Kerry closed her eyes, imagining the warm strength of Theo's arms around her. Being in his arms always felt so right. Just now, even when he was worried about his nephew and his sister-in-law, he had taken a moment to give her comfort and reassurance.

He had told her that she'd done the right thing— except he didn't know what had really happened. What she had really done.

She walked shakily across to the window and looked

out at the city, which was now properly dark. Somewhere out there Corban was pursuing his wife and child. And Theo was helping him. She squeezed her eyes shut, feeling a tear escape to run down her cheek, and prayed that everyone would be all right.

Theo Diakos strode through the hotel with a face like thunder. Hallie and the child had been safely retrieved by his brother, but not before she had crashed her car on Syntagma Square.

Mercifully no one had been injured—but driving a sports car off the road on one of the busiest squares in Athens, right outside the parliament building, had attracted a deluge of unwanted attention, and a horde of paparazzi had appeared out of nowhere before Corban had been able to get his family away from prying eyes.

Theo swore under his breath. If only he had persuaded his brother to act sooner—to get Hallie out of the country and away from the family—then none of this would have happened. It had been becoming increasingly difficult to keep Hallie's drinking problem under wraps, and this fiasco would certainly blow it wide open.

Up until that evening almost no one had known about her difficulty with alcohol. Even Kerry—as far as he knew—had remained unaware. Corban had worked hard to keep it a secret—but now everyone would know.

Theo glanced at his watch. Only a few minutes had passed since he'd called Kerry to tell her that the situation was contained, but she had sounded so distressed by the whole event that he wanted to get back to her without delay. He was sorry that she'd been dragged into such an unpleasant family situation. Witnessing Hallie drunk and out of control, then putting Nicco at risk and creating an unsavoury public embarrassment, had obviously been upsetting for her.

Kerry would never behave like that. There wasn't a disagreeable bone in her body. She was gentle and graceful, and she hated drawing attention to herself. Theo valued every minute he spent in her enchanting company.

He'd first spotted her nearly a year earlier, talking to a group of tourists in the foyer of one of his hotels. Her long blonde hair, wide blue eyes and honeyed complexion had initially caught his attention, but once he'd spent an evening with her it had been her gentle charm that had utterly captivated him. After the cut and thrust of his high-paced business life, time with Kerry was the perfect refreshing antidote.

Now he was hurrying back to her, waiting for him on the roof garden. He knew how much she loved it there, and he hoped the pleasant surroundings would ease her distress. But if she was still upset when he reached her, he would pull her into his arms and make love to her until she forgot her worries.

He found her standing with her back to him, looking out over the city towards the Acropolis. The second he took another step towards her she seemed to sense his presence and spun round to face him, her hair bouncing about her shoulders as she moved.

'Is everyone all right?' she asked urgently. 'Hallie and Nicco? People on the street where she crashed?'

'Everyone is fine,' Theo said. He pulled her towards him, but her body was filled with tension and she didn't sway into his arms as he had expected. He leant closer, swept her silky hair away from her neck and pressed his lips to the sensitive skin below her ear. 'Forget about it now—it's all under control. Let me take your mind off your worries.'

'Where are they now?' Kerry asked, standing even straighter and stiffer than before. 'Are they all together?'

Theo stepped back and looked down at her. In the time they'd been together Kerry had never once refused his lovemaking. She was so deliciously responsive to him that it made sex even more exciting and satisfying for him. Even thinking about the way she dissolved into a pool of desire at his slightest touch made him hot and ready for her.

Usually a simple look from him was enough to have her melting willingly into his arms. For her to be so immune to him she must be really concerned.

'Yes. Corban has everything under control. At any moment they will be flying out to the island—away from the press,' Theo said, skimming his hands up the bare skin of her arms with the lightest of touches. 'You can stop worrying about them now—and let me make you feel better.'

Kerry stood tall and drew in a deep breath. She had to talk to Theo—to tell him what she had done. And she had to ask about the conversation she'd overheard him having with Corban.

Then, after that, she still had to tell him she was

pregnant. It was almost impossible to believe that only a couple of hours ago she had been running to tell Theo the amazing news that they were going to have a baby—and then everything suddenly seemed to become horribly confusing and wrong.

'Let me see if I can think of something new…something interesting,' Theo said, his voice deep and sexy, as he reached out to pluck a couple of beautiful pink roses from the trellis beside them.

Kerry drew in a wobbly breath and looked at the gorgeous blooms in Theo's large, sensual hands. Only last night he had carried her out to the roof garden from their bedroom, peeled off her lacy nightclothes and laid her naked under the stars. Then he'd scattered her body with rose petals before making long, slow, exquisite love to her.

Now the heady fragrance of roses was already filling her senses again, and her body was burning with the need to surrender to his lovemaking. She knew that she would soon forget everything in the bliss that he would give her.

But she couldn't surrender to her desires. It wasn't right when there were still so many concerns in her mind. She had to talk to him.

'Stop. I need to…' She hesitated, then pushed his hands away and took a step backwards. 'Earlier this evening I heard you talking to Corban. You said he was to take Nicco away from Hallie.'

'Yes. It's a shame I didn't give my brother that advice yesterday,' Theo replied. 'Then tonight's fiasco would have been avoided.'

'How can you be so cold?' Kerry gasped. 'Someone could have been seriously hurt tonight—or even killed!'

'Exactly,' Theo said. 'That could have been averted.'

'Not by depriving a mother of her child,' Kerry said.

For a moment she couldn't help thinking about her own mother—how she'd been utterly devastated to have had her baby taken away from her. Feeling like a worthless failure at only sixteen years old had made it impossible for her to get herself back on track. Her life had spiralled into depression and self-abuse. She'd turned to drink, then drugs—and eventually died alone of an overdose in squalid conditions.

For Kerry it was made worse by the fact that she hadn't even known who her mother was until it was too late to help her. Instead she'd been grudgingly looked after by her grandmother—the very person who had taken her away from her real mother. And for Kerry's entire childhood she'd made her feel unwanted and unloved.

'I know you are concerned about Hallie and Nicco.' Theo's clipped tones showed signs of tension. 'My brother and I are in your debt for raising the alarm—if you hadn't come to us so quickly things could have been much worse. But my conversation with Corban was private. How we choose to take care of our family is none of your concern.'

Kerry stared up at him. A muscle pulsed on his shadowed jawline. His eyes were dark and troubled. She had to tell him what she had done—but she was apprehensive about how he would react.

'Hallie is my friend,' she said. 'Of course I care about her. And Nicco.'

'You must trust me to do what is right for my family,' Theo said, studying her intently. Suddenly his eyes narrowed and the set of his expression hardened.

'You told her. Didn't you?' he demanded.

Kerry's heart jolted and her eyes widened with alarm.

'Yes.' Her voice was hardly more than a whisper—but she held her head up and met his gaze steadily.

'You had no business doing that.' Theo's expression was dark. 'It did not concern you.'

'Of course it concerned me!' Kerry responded, suddenly filled with anger on her friend's behalf—and on her own mother's behalf.

'No wonder you were so desperately worried—your actions put many people in danger tonight,' he said. 'Someone could have died. My nephew could have died!'

'I didn't realise she'd been drinking,' Kerry said. 'Not until—'

'Don't try to explain what you did.' Theo's voice cut through hers coldly. 'I'm not interested.'

'But—'

'I'm not interested in your excuses,' he said flatly. 'You put my nephew in danger.'

'I never meant to,' she said. 'That was the last thing I wanted.'

'You listened to a private conversation that did not concern you,' he said. 'Then you went behind my back and took the situation into your own hands.'

'Hallie is my friend,' she said.

'And what am *I* to you?' he demanded. 'You should have come to me first.'

'You… I…' She stumbled hesitantly, suddenly unsure of herself.

It was true that if she'd spoken to Theo about what she'd overheard then Hallie wouldn't have taken Nicco in the car. But that didn't change what she had heard. And Theo had made it clear that he saw nothing wrong with what he and his brother had been planning. They probably still intended to take Nicco away from his mother.

'I no longer want you here.' Theo spoke suddenly, his voice hard and controlled, his expression set in stone. 'Pack your bags and get out.'

'What? I don't understand…' Kerry's voice trailed away and she stared at him in shock. But she did understand. Theo no longer wanted her.

He'd already turned his back on her and was walking away, as if from that moment she was dead to him. She was already out of his life.

'Wait,' she called. 'There is something I have to tell you. It's the reason I came to talk to you in your study in the first place.'

Theo spun on his heel and looked at her dispassionately. He was giving her a moment more of his time, and she knew she had to use it wisely.

'This evening I found out—'

Kerry stopped speaking abruptly and covered her mouth with her hand. Suddenly she was afraid to tell him that she was pregnant.

After the events of the evening, it was almost as if

Theo was a different man. She would never have thought him capable of taking a child from his mother—but he had defended his intentions even when Kerry had challenged him.

And if they planned to do that to Hallie—who'd been married to Corban for several years—what would happen to *her* if they found out she was carrying a Diakos baby? Theo had made it plain he didn't want her. But would he want to take the baby?

'Get on with it,' Theo said, with undisguised impatience.

'I don't feel like I know you any more,' she said.

'The feeling is mutual,' he replied coldly. 'Now, get out.'

CHAPTER TWO

14 months later

'THANK you for inviting me to your home.' Theo held out his hand to the old man, who was sitting at a small wooden table drinking coffee under the shade of an ancient gnarled olive tree. 'Your island is charming—a very peaceful place to live.'

Drakon Notara ignored Theo's hand and snorted rudely, not looking up from his treacly Greek coffee. He was a moody and eccentric old man, but Theo had met him several times in Athens and was not fazed by his bad manners.

'Don't tell me you care about *peace*,' Drakon said. 'I know why you want to buy my island. You want to build one of your flashy hotels here—or maybe several. Bars, thumping music, people drunk and rowdy.' He paused, finally lifting his head and meeting Theo's eye. 'I can't have that happening here.'

Theo gritted his teeth and stared straight back, refusing to rise to the old man's provocation. No one spoke to Theo Diakos with such disrespect and got away with it—but he had a compelling reason to do business with Drakon Notara.

Theo *needed* to buy this island. It was his only chance to fulfil his mother's dying wish. And if he had to tread carefully to seal the deal, then that was what he would do.

He had not been invited to sit, nor offered any refreshment. The paving stones under the trees had not been swept before his arrival and were deep with browning piles of olive blossom. It was clear the old man was going to be as bloody-minded as usual, and was not going to make any transaction easy.

'That's not what I intend for the island at all,' Theo said smoothly. 'Perhaps if we talk—'

'No,' Drakon barked. 'Talk is cheap. And so are the scandal sheets. Don't think because I spend most of my time out here that I don't know what your family is like—rich and spoiled, caring only about money and excitement. Your brother…his drunken wife crashing her car with that child on board.'

'You have been misinformed.' Theo's tone was clipped as he suppressed the surge of anger that ripped through him. Whenever he thought about the night of the accident, which was over a year ago now, he felt his temper flare. 'My family is not as the media has portrayed it. The newspapers do not always report things exactly as they are.'

'Are you telling me it didn't happen?' the old man scoffed.

'I'm saying that my personal affairs are not relevant

to our business,' Theo said. 'However, if you will allow me to set out my proposal, I believe we will be able to come to an arrangement we are both happy with.'

'I don't want to talk to you now—I don't want to hear the smooth and readymade business spiel you have prepared.' Drakon leant heavily on the table and levered himself up. 'If you're serious about buying my island, come and stay for a few days—so I can find out what kind of man you really are. Bring your pretty girl-friend—the one I met last year. I liked her—no airs and graces, which I found surprising in someone associated with you and your family.'

For a fraction of a second Theo did not reply. The wily old fellow had completely wrong-footed him. He searched his memory, trying to recall any occasions when Kerry and Drakon might have met—and realised there had been several charity events when they could have spoken.

Why did Drakon really want him to bring Kerry to the island? Did he know that she was no longer part of his life?

'Or have you broken it off with her? Moved on to someone new?' Drakon continued derisively. 'From the way she…' He paused, frowning as if he was irritated with himself. 'What was her name?'

'Kerry,' Theo supplied in a tight voice, not missing the fact that Drakon had used the past tense—as if he definitely *did* know the relationship was over. 'Her name *is* Kerry.'

Hearing himself say her name sounded strange and painfully familiar at the same time. He had not said it aloud since the night he threw her out—but that had not stopped her name, and the image of her face, pressing forward in his thoughts more often than he would have liked.

'Ah, yes. Kerry,' Drakon said. 'Utterly delightful young thing—reminded me of my dear wife when she was young. From the way she never left your side, I expected to see a wedding announcement in the press. But I suppose you're several women down the line by now.' He turned and started shuffling towards the house.

'As I said, my personal affairs are not relevant to our business,' Theo said, but a cold, fatalistic feeling had settled in his chest.

He realised that as far as Drakon Notara was concerned the way he conducted his private life was as important as the way he did business. The fact that not one single woman had caught his attention since Kerry would not impress the old man. He would simply judge Theo harshly for not making the relationship work in the first place.

And, to make matters worse, he seemed to have developed a real soft spot for Kerry.

'I'm a traditional old man,' Drakon said over his shoulder. 'I don't hold with the fast and wasteful way people live their lives these days. Fast cars polluting the air, fast relationships…everything is disposable.'

'If we talk, you'll discover that we share many of the same traditional values,' Theo said.

He wanted to follow Drakon and convince him that he did not plan to build hotels on the island. But his reasons for wanting the island were personal and he had no intention of sharing them with anyone—especially not a judgemental old man who thought it was his right to force his opinions on other people.

'Then come back and visit properly,' Drakon said, pausing on the threshold, as if to gather his strength before he disappeared inside. 'And bring Kerry with you.'

Theo watched him go. He might be physically frail, but his mind and his will were still as strong as ever.

'Allow me to escort you back to the helipad,' Drakon's assistant said, stepping out of the shadows at the edge of the paved area.

Theo nodded a curt acknowledgement, and turned to leave.

'I know the way,' he said, striding out of the shaded area into the bright Greek sunshine.

He frowned as he walked along the rutted ridge path, completely oblivious to the breathtaking view across the azure Aegean Sea.

He needed Kerry.

If he was to have any chance of buying this island as the first step in fulfilling his mother's dying wish, then he was going to need Kerry.

'Thank you so much for all your help,' the customer said, pushing open the glass door of the travel agent's and letting in a blast of cold, rainy air.

'I'm sure you'll have a wonderful holiday. I've only been to Crete once, but I'd love to go back there,' Kerry said, as the customer stepped out onto the wet street.

For a brief moment she let herself imagine how good it would feel to sit on a beautiful sandy beach, with nothing to do but rest and play with her six-month-old baby boy, Lucas. But that was a fantasy that wasn't likely to come true any time soon—not with all the bills she was struggling to pay on her own.

It was fourteen months since she'd returned from Athens—since the devastating night when Theo Diakos had brutally ripped out her heart and trampled it underfoot. Arriving back in London had been a nightmare. Trying to pick up the pieces of her broken heart—with no job, no money and nowhere to live—had been truly awful. And on top of everything else she'd been pregnant.

'It's nearly time for your break,' Carol said now, pulling her out of her thoughts. 'Are you sure you don't mind taking early lunch again?'

'When you've been up since five a.m., this doesn't seem early.' Kerry laughed. Lucas—as adorable as he was—had taken to waking with the rising sun.

At that moment the shop door opened again, and another blast of cold air whooshed in, making an icy shiver run through her.

'Ooh! I can't believe it's June already,' she said, as she pulled the collar of her uniform jacket more snugly across her throat and looked up to greet the customer who had just walked in. 'Good morning. Can I help—?'

Her heart skipped a beat and she felt herself go cold all over as she stared up into the face of Theo Diakos.

He was looking straight at her, with an expression of dispassionate assessment on his darkly handsome face.

His black brows were drawn low, casting his eyes into shadow, but his penetrating eyes bored right into her.

Kerry drew in a shaky breath and felt her heart jolt painfully back into action. She knew she was staring—but she could not drag her eyes from him. If was as if she couldn't quite believe Theo Diakos was really standing there.

He was a tall and imposing figure. The size of his athletic body seemed to fill the entire doorway, and his magnetic presence seemed to fill the entire shop. He was wearing a dark suit, which was covered with a sheen of summer rain, and his black hair was damp and glistening with fine water droplets.

What was he doing here?

Had he found out about Lucas—his baby son?

'Can I offer you some assistance?' Carol asked, breaking the silence and walking around to the front of her desk. 'Would you like to see a particular brochure, or are you just at the ideas-collecting stage?'

A flash of almost feverish humour cut through Kerry like a sharp slap to knock her out of her stunned state. The idea of Theo Diakos—billionaire property tycoon—walking into a high street travel agency in a London backwater to book his next package holiday was laughable. Ludicrous, even.

No—he was here for a reason.

'I'm here to speak to Kerry,' Theo said, never taking his eyes off her for a second.

'Oh. You two know each other?' Carol paused, obviously surprised, and looked at Kerry questioningly.

She was still staring at Theo. He was so familiar, but at the same time like a total stranger.

She had been so utterly in love with him—but it had turned out she'd meant nothing to him. Nothing at all. In one horrifying evening she had discovered that his soul was made of stone, and that there was not even one ounce of compassion inside his hard, unyielding body.

He'd conspired with his brother to take a little child away from his mother. And when Kerry had made the mistake of getting involved he had not given her an opportunity to explain herself. It had been the first time in nearly a year that they'd had any sort of disagreement—but he'd simply thrown her out. Without a moment's hesitation.

'Carol, this is Theo. He is from Athens.' Kerry's natural politeness forced her to make at least some sort of introduction—but all her instincts told her not to say too much. No one at work knew anything about what had happened in Athens, and it paid to be as careful as possible. She didn't want any speculation about Lucas and who his father was.

'Why don't you go for your lunch break?' Carol suggested. 'You probably have lots to catch up on.'

Kerry's pulse was still racing and the palms of her hands suddenly felt damp. The last thing she wanted was to go off alone with Theo—but neither did she want to cause a stir at work. Her boss, Margaret, would be back from her emergency dental appointment soon, and chances were she would not be in a good mood. Kerry really needed her job, and she really did not want to give anyone fuel for gossip.

'All right. I'll get my bag.' She stood up and walked to the office at the back of the shop, desperately hoping that she didn't look as wobbly as she suddenly felt.

With every thump of her heart she felt Theo's gaze burning deeper and deeper into her—through the protective veneer of her uniform, piercing through all the emotional barricades she had tried to build up since that devastating night in Athens.

Why was he here?

The office door swung shut behind her, shielding her from his sight, and her legs buckled beneath her. She clung to the edge of the desk, gasping for air and shaking violently.

Had Theo come to try and take Lucas away from her?

She'd never let that happen—her gorgeous boy was everything to her. She loved him more than life itself, and she'd never, *never* let Theo take him.

She took a deep, steadying breath and looked back through the one-way mirror into the shop. Theo was still standing there, as inscrutable as an ancient Greek statue, and Carol was obviously trying to engage him in conversation.

The sudden, horrifying thought occurred to her that Carol might innocently mention Lucas. With another judder of her already painful heart she grabbed her bag and burst back through the door. She had to get Theo away from anyone who knew her as quickly as possible.

'Take as long as you want,' Carol said, trying to be helpful. 'I'll send you a sneaky text if Margaret gets back.'

'I won't be long,' Kerry said.

'Don't worry,' Carol said. 'Have fun. Enjoy your blast from the past.'

'Thanks.' Kerry slipped past Theo and pushed the heavy glass door open. She flashed her colleague a tight smile and walked away down the rainy street, leaving Theo to follow her.

Fun was the last thing she was expecting to have. And as for Carol's unsuspecting use of the phrase *blast from the past*—all Kerry could think about was the more violent, destructive meaning of the word *blast*.

She desperately hoped Theo hadn't come to rip mercilessly through her life, laying everything to waste and destroying the tentative happiness she had finally found.

Suddenly she couldn't bear the agony of not knowing. She stopped abruptly and turned to face Theo.

'What are you doing here?' she demanded.

'I've come to take you back to Greece,' he said.

CHAPTER THREE

THEO stood still, watching Kerry's reaction to his announcement. For a second he hardly recognised her. Somehow she didn't seem like the woman he'd spent nearly a year of his life with.

There were the obvious differences—the unflattering navy blue uniform, and the new way she had done her blonde hair, twisting it up into a tight knot at the nape of her neck with a long fringe he didn't remember falling into her eyes. But the real differences seemed to be deeper, more profound than that. She looked older in some way, and the expression on her face was wary and troubled.

He frowned, momentarily disconcerted as he looked down into her eyes. He could have sworn that her eyes had been a soft clear blue, but now they appeared to be pale grey, as if they were reflecting the pastel colour of the rain-streaked sky.

'Why would you say that?' Kerry gasped. 'I'm not coming back to Greece with you.'

'Actually, you are,' Theo said.

'Why?' she demanded incredulously. 'Why do you want me to? And what makes you think I'd ever go anywhere with you ever again?'

'Because you owe me that,' he replied.

'I don't owe you anything!' Kerry exclaimed, anger suddenly flaring inside her. 'I gave up my career to be with you, and I never took any of the money you tried to give me. I used up all my savings while I was living with you, which made it really hard for me when I came back to London.'

She paused, racking her brain for any other possible reason he might think that she owed him. The very idea that he could want anything of her was ridiculous—he was one of the richest men in Athens.

'I left all the expensive jewellery you gave me behind,' she added, remembering how much that had hurt.

It wasn't because of the cost of the items—for Kerry their value had been entirely sentimental. She'd thought they were genuine tokens of Theo's affection for her. When he'd thrown her out so coldly, she'd realised that all the things she'd taken as meaningful in their relationship had obviously meant nothing at all to him.

'I'm not talking about trivial monetary matters,' Theo said flatly.

'Then what—?' Kerry's voice dried up in her throat. Did that mean he *had* found out about Lucas?

She bit her lip, desperately hoping that he hadn't discovered her secret. Surely he would have brought up something so important immediately? But perhaps he meant to string it out to torment her.

'You interfered with matters that did not concern you,' Theo said. 'The consequences could have been tragic.'

Kerry drew in a shaky breath, remembering the awful evening of the accident.

'No one was injured,' she said in a small voice.

She deeply regretted that her involvement had caused Hallie to drive off with Nicco when she'd been drinking. But that did not change the fact that Theo and Corban had been planning to take Nicco away from his mother.

'It's a miracle no one was killed,' Theo said. 'But that's not exactly the reason I'm here.'

Kerry stared up at him anxiously. What could be worse than causing a potential tragedy—something bad enough to bring Theo all the way from Athens to seek restitution from her?

'Your meddling stirred up a vicious media circus,' Theo said, as if that was on the same level as a tragedy. 'The paparazzi had a field-day. They hounded my family relentlessly—Hallie and Corban in particular. It made things very difficult.'

Relief that Theo had not come about Lucas poured through Kerry—making her bold. Was he *really* comparing the inconvenience of unwanted media interest with the possibility of someone dying in a car crash? How had she ever lived with this man—shared his home for six months—without realising what he was really like?

'You mean with the media watching everything you did it made it difficult for you to take your sister-in-law's child away from her?' she asked.

As soon as the words were out of her mouth she

knew she should not have antagonised him. A change came over him that made goosebumps prickle across her skin. It was hard to pinpoint what was actually different about his expression or his body language, but something alerted her to danger.

'It would be better—*for you*—if you never mention what you overheard that night again.'

Theo's voice grated across her nerves, making her heart start to race once more. But then all of a sudden her hackles rose at the threat in his tone. How dared he tell her what to do? She wasn't in a relationship with him any more.

'Why not? Are you ashamed of yourself for contemplating something so horrible?' she demanded recklessly. 'Or are you simply lying low—intending to carry on with your plan once the heat is off?'

Theo glared down at her, his blood suddenly surging hot and angry through his veins. He'd had no idea that Kerry had it in her to behave like this. The woman who'd been his lover for nearly a year would never have been so hot-headed, never have challenged him so rashly.

'Be very careful,' he grated, stepping forward so that he towered over her, forcing her to crane her neck back to maintain eye contact.

'Why?' she demanded, planting her hands on her hips and refusing to back away. 'What are you going to do to me?'

Theo could almost feel the energy crackling between them. Despite the cool air of the wet summer day, there was real heat in the space around their bodies. It was the heat of anger—and it was far more than just that.

It was the heat of passion—emotional and sexual.

Suddenly he knew exactly what he wanted to do to her, and it took every ounce of his self-control not to give in to his desires. The need to seize her in his arms and drag her hard against his body was almost overwhelming. He wanted to cover her angry mouth with his—to silence her in the most satisfying way he knew how.

He continued to stare down at her, letting the silence lengthen. His heart was pumping powerfully in his chest, and his body was thrumming with desire for her. Then he saw her eyes widen slightly, saw her lips part a little as her breathing deepened. And he knew she felt it too.

Pure physical attraction.

A few minutes earlier it had seemed as if he didn't know her any more—but now he knew precisely how her body was reacting to him. After all, they had been lovers for nearly a year. He recognised the heat suddenly dancing in her cheeks, and the way her pupils had grown large in her pale-coloured eyes.

She wanted him as much as he wanted her.

Suddenly he gripped her arms and pulled her towards him, up onto her tiptoes so that her lips were just below his. All he had to do was bend his head a fraction more and his mouth would come down over hers. He would take back what had once been his—reclaim her body in hot, hard retribution for what she had done.

But this wasn't what he had come to London for. He could not—*would* not—let his libido get in the way of fulfilling his mother's dying wish. He needed Kerry to convince Drakon to sell him the island.

'I didn't come here for this,' he said gruffly, letting go of her arms and stepping away from her.

'I don't know what you mean,' Kerry said, shaken by how husky her voice sounded.

How had she let herself fall under his sensual spell so easily? Why would she even respond to him at all, after the horrible way he had treated her?

'You know as well as I do,' he said. 'Let's not play any more games. I'll tell you what I came for.'

'Why don't you?' she said, pleased with how sassy she managed to sound, considering the way her body was still buzzing with unwanted desire for him. Even though her face was streaked with rain, she could feel her cheeks burning. 'It's taking you long enough to get round to it.'

The rain was coming down more heavily now, and she lifted her hand to brush her long wet fringe back from her face. She stared straight up into his eyes, determined not to let him see any weakness. She'd be ready next time, if he started looking at her like that again—as if he wanted to tear off her clothes and make love to her right there and then.

After everything that had happened she couldn't believe he'd had the audacity to come on to her like that. And she couldn't believe she'd let herself respond. She would not let it happen again.

'Do you want to go inside?' he asked, glancing around as if he was looking for a café. 'Sit out of the rain while we talk?'

'No. I'm already wet, and my break is nearly over,' she said. 'Just tell me what you want from me.'

She didn't relish the idea of continuing their conversation standing in the rain on a busy urban pavement—but somehow she felt safer out in the open. The thought of being in a confined space with him, even a public café, sent a shiver of apprehension down her spine.

'I want to buy an island from an old man,' Theo said, getting straight to the point. 'I need *you* to help me secure the deal.'

Kerry frowned up at him. She felt slightly startled by the fact that he was finally being direct about his reason for coming to her, but she was also puzzled as to why he thought he needed *her* help.

'What have I got to do with it?' she asked, intrigued despite herself.

'It is because *you* meddled in my family's affairs—creating a situation that caused the media frenzy—that the old man is reluctant to do business with me,' Theo said. 'He wants to sell his island to someone with traditional values—someone he approves of.'

'I don't understand how you think I can help you—even if I wanted to,' Kerry said. 'What can *I* do to change the way this man thinks about you?'

'The old man in question is called Drakon Notara. He remembers meeting you. Apparently he liked you,' Theo replied, somehow making it sound as if he thought it highly unlikely that *anyone* would actually like her.

'I remember him.' Kerry frowned, irritated by Theo's tone. 'He told me all about the wildlife sanctuary he has on his island. He hates all these intensive modern developments and wants to keep somewhere natural.' She paused and looked at Theo quizzically. 'Why do *you* want to buy a wildlife sanctuary?'

For a long moment he didn't respond, and something made Kerry think that Theo hadn't even known about the sanctuary. He just wanted the island.

'No wonder Drakon doesn't want to sell to you,' she said. 'He doesn't want a hotel on his nature preserve.'

'It seemed to me that he was more concerned with my commitment to family values,' Theo said curtly. 'Therefore you will accompany me to his island tomorrow—travelling as my fiancée. At no point will you reveal that we have not been together since you met him.'

Kerry stared at him in shock.

'Fiancée?' she repeated.

For a moment she almost thought he was proposing to her. But that would be crazy. Almost as crazy as him expecting a woman he'd heartlessly cast aside for making one mistake to pose as his fiancée. Just so that he could buy an island from an old man who apparently did not approve of him.

'Yes,' Theo said. 'For the duration of the few days we are to spend on the island you are to act the perfect, adoring fiancée in every way.'

'I wasn't your fiancée when I met Drakon,' she said, saying the first thing that came into her mind. It seemed a ridiculous thing to say—but so was the charade Theo was suggesting.

'Time has passed since then,' Theo said. 'It would seem natural that our relationship has progressed.'

'Progressed!' Kerry exclaimed, finally coming to her

senses. 'That's an interesting take on it. I thought it had ended—badly—the night you kicked me out without giving me a chance to defend myself.'

'There's no defence for what you did,' Theo said. 'So why would I listen to whatever spin you wanted to put on your meddling? Whatever excuse you were going to give me?'

'There's no way I'm going to help you persuade a dear old man to sell you his island,' she said.

'Yes, you are,' Theo said. 'I will collect you from your flat tomorrow morning.'

'You don't know where I live!' she exclaimed.

'Of course I do,' he replied scathingly. 'Be packed and ready by six-thirty.'

Biting panic suddenly flared within her—freezing her insides stone-cold with dread. He'd found out where she worked, which probably meant he *did* know where she lived. And if he knew that, what else had his people found out about her—what else would they find if they dug deeper?

She had to keep Lucas hidden from him.

She remembered his words—*a Diakos child belongs with the Diakos family.*

He'd had no qualms about taking Hallie's child from her, and she was married to his brother—a true member of the family. What chance did Kerry have against him if he wanted to take his son?

'Don't make me come for you at work tomorrow,' Theo said. 'I will find you if you try to hide from me. And if you give me the runaround I will not be pleased.'

* * *

Kerry stood on the pavement outside her block of flats at six o'clock the following morning. It was very early, but she could not risk Theo coming inside the building to look for her. The closer she let him come to her home, the more chance there was of him finding out about Lucas.

Half an hour later, when a smart black limousine pulled up beside her, she discovered that she'd be travelling alone. Theo had already returned to Athens the previous evening.

'Your ticket, Miss Martin,' his assistant said, handing her a white envelope. 'You are booked on a flight out of Heathrow airport this morning. You will be met when you arrive in Athens, and taken to join Mr Diakos. You will then fly out to the island together.'

'Thank you,' Kerry said automatically. Still slightly stunned by Theo's absence, she slipped into the limo and stared out through the tinted window.

Was Theo really so confident that she would meekly do as she was told? She'd never actually agreed to go with him. In fact she'd told him point-blank that she was not going. Had she always been so biddable that it just didn't occur to him that she might refuse to co-operate?

He didn't know the reason she'd had to go—the secret she could not risk him uncovering if she made him come looking for her. He must simply have expected her to do as she was told because that was what she had always done.

She closed her eyes and hugged herself, already missing Lucas although it was scarcely an hour since she'd left him with Bridget—the only person in the world she truly trusted. They'd been brought up together as sisters and, despite the fact that she had discovered later that Bridget was really her aunt, they still shared an incredibly close, sisterly bond.

Kerry knew Lucas would be safe with her. Bridget had her own little ones and was used to babies, but even so Kerry felt horrible leaving him. She knew she had no choice—to protect her son she had to leave him for a couple of nights—but somehow she felt she was letting him down.

Theo glanced across at Kerry as they climbed out of the helicopter on Drakon Notara's island. Her hair was whipping about in the wind, and as she put up her hands to hold it back from her face he saw that she was pale and shaky after the flight.

She'd never complained, even though he'd asked her to join him on many of his trips, but Theo knew she wasn't a good traveller. Chances were she hadn't slept much the night before, and the limo had picked her up very early that morning. Tiredness always made her travel sickness worse, and he guessed she was feeling pretty rough. But he wanted her bright and appealing, to convince Drakon to sell him the island.

'I know the way to the house,' he said, as the old man's quirky assistant came towards them. 'My fiancée needs a moment to recover from the journey—some fresh air and solid ground under her feet for a while will do the trick.'

He reached out, looped his arm around her waist and

pulled her close to him. He felt a tremor pass through her as she tensed and tried to pull away from him.

'Lean on me till you get your strength back,' Theo said, tightening his hold on her. Then he dropped his voice and spoke quietly, for her ears alone. 'Don't forget why you are here. You are my fiancée and you will act like it.'

With a deliberate effort Kerry relaxed her body and allowed herself to lean against Theo. She was surprised that apparently he'd picked up on how she was feeling— he'd never shown any sign of noticing her tendency to motion sickness before. But this time it *was* particularly awful—probably almost anyone would have noticed if she looked even half as bad as she felt.

All she could do was concentrate on drawing calming breaths into her lungs and putting one foot in front of the other. Theo's arm was around her—a steady anchor and a welcome distraction from the nausea that rolled through her.

However, it didn't take long before her awareness shifted entirely onto the sensation of his hard body next to her. The stressful journey and the way it had made her feel so rotten slipped away, and she was simply conscious of how closely Theo was holding her.

His body was strong and athletic, and she could feel his muscles moving as they made their way along the rocky path together. They were walking in unison, and she suddenly realised that meant he had matched his stride to hers. For some reason that realisation sent a shiver skittering down her spine. Whether it had been intentional or instinctive, on some level Theo had been attuned to her body and the rhythm of her movements.

'Feeling better now?' he asked. His deep, masculine voice passed like a physical vibration right through her, setting her nerve-endings alight and making her even more conscious of his powerful male form beside her.

She turned to look up at him, suddenly convinced that he had known the exact moment her attention had shifted onto the sensual experience of walking with him. Somehow the thought made her feel exposed and vulnerable.

She lifted her head and his eyes caught hers, holding them locked to his dark gaze. He was studying her intently, and all at once she got the feeling that he was probing—trying to read her mind. She didn't remember him looking at her like that before—as if he thought she was guilty of something.

Then she suddenly realised that she'd never had anything to hide from him before. Was she imagining his scrutiny because she had an enormous secret?

'The house is just over the brow of the hill,' he said, lifting his hands to cradle her face gently. 'Drakon may be old—but his mind is sharp. He'll be watching us, so never let the pretence that you are my fiancée slip.'

'I don't want to lie,' she said, pulling away from him slightly. She'd enjoyed meeting Drakon the previous year, and, despite his funny old ways, she had liked him. 'It doesn't feel right.'

'Then we'd better make our act convincing, so

Drakon won't ask you any tricky questions,' Theo said. 'And, as they say, actions speak louder than words.'

Before she realised his intention, one strong arm had slipped around her back and pulled her hard against him. The other hand lifted to cup her chin and tip her face up to his.

She opened her lips to protest, and at that moment his mouth came down on hers.

CHAPTER FOUR

THEO'S kiss took Kerry completely by surprise, but her body responded instinctively. It seemed the most natural thing in the world for her to lean into him, pressing sensuously against his hard, athletic body, and part her lips in invitation.

His tongue swept into her mouth, hot and demanding, and she felt herself become molten with longing. There was nothing tender about his kiss—it was a fierce and passionate reminder of all the times they had made love. Of all the times he'd taken her to the point of ecstasy.

She lifted her own tongue to meet his, surrendering to the intense desire that suddenly stormed through her body, and kissed him back wildly. Her hands ran up to his shoulders, revelling in the hot, hard feel of his muscles, and she clung to him tightly—as if she never wanted to let go.

Then, without warning, Theo broke away from the kiss.

Kerry gasped in surprise, swaying unsteadily as he abruptly released his hold on her.

'Quite convincing,' he said, as he stepped away and stared down at her through narrowed eyes.

She held her breath as she looked up into his face, and for a moment the world stood still. She'd dreamed of Theo kissing her again for more than a year—but in her fantasy he had been kissing her because he had realised his mistake, realised that he loved her.

Her dream had never been like this—her kissing him desperately, with embarrassing eagerness. And with him appearing to be completely unmoved by the whole thing.

She felt the hot colour of humiliation staining her cheeks, and she looked down at the ground, mortified that she had given herself away so completely. Then a wave of anger rose through her, and her eyes snapped back up to meet his.

'It was my intention to be convincing,' she said. 'But there'll be no more free demonstrations. I'm here to help you with Drakon—not to be nice to you in private.'

Theo raised his straight black brows in surprise, but his lips quirked in amusement, and she had the feeling he'd seen right through her.

'Let's go and meet our host,' he said, sliding his arm around her waist and turning to continue along the path.

'I understand you weren't feeling too well when you arrived,' Drakon said, looking across the table at Kerry with sharp eyes. 'I trust you're feeling better now?'

'Yes, I'm fine,' she said. 'Thank you for asking.' She took a sip of her drink and smiled across at him. It was lovely sitting outside under the shade of the twisted old olive trees, enjoying the stunning view over the bay to the Adriatic. And making small talk with Drakon stopped her thinking about what had happened with Theo on the path from the helipad.

'Kerry suffers from travel sickness,' Theo said, taking her by surprise. She'd assumed he'd only guessed how she'd felt earlier because she had looked particularly rough. She'd never realised that he'd always known that she often felt ill on long journeys. 'After a short rest she's usually back to normal,' he added.

'What a nuisance travel sickness must be,' Drakon said. 'Especially when you travel such a lot.'

'Don't make me feel bad.' Theo's tone was wry. 'Even though I know she suffers, I ask her to come with me because I can't bear to be without her.'

'Love is selfish sometimes,' Drakon said, knocking back a huge swallow of ouzo.

'It can be.' Theo turned his piercing gaze onto Kerry.

A strange feeling washed over her as his dark eyes found hers, and suddenly she couldn't maintain eye contact with him. She took another sip of her drink, hoping to cover up how disconcerted she felt. The direction the conversation had taken had knocked her totally off balance.

When they'd been together Theo had told her the same thing—that he wanted her to travel with him because he couldn't bear to be without her. At the time his words had made her feel special—valued. Never before in her life had anyone shown so much desire to have her around.

She'd grown up feeling unwanted and unloved—and when she was eighteen years old she'd found out just how true that was. Her grandmother had not wanted to care for her, but had grudgingly become her guardian out of a twisted sense of duty, having refused to accept that her teenage daughter was capable of looking after her own baby.

But it had turned out that Theo hadn't genuinely valued her company either. She'd made one mistake—and then he couldn't get rid of her fast enough. Drakon's mention of love being selfish was just another cruel reminder of how little she'd meant to Theo. He'd never loved her and she knew he never would.

'I hope that tomorrow you will allow us to view the whole island,' Theo said to their host, pulling Kerry out of her thoughts.

'No business talk now.' Drakon waved away his request and looked at Kerry. 'My dear, I haven't seen you for such a long time. I know I don't leave the island much, but there were a couple of occasions in Athens when I was hoping to meet you again.'

'Oh, I'm sorry,' Kerry said, feeling a knot of tension tighten in her stomach as she found herself on the spot. She did not want to think about how Theo would react if she failed to convince Drakon that they were still together. 'Unfortunately I haven't been able to accompany Theo to every event lately,' she continued. 'I've been spending a lot of time in London—I've had family commitments.'

She pushed her long fringe out of her eyes and thought about Lucas. She was completely and utterly committed to her baby boy, and would do anything for him. Unlike her own mother—who had been too young and too weak when Kerry was born, and had not managed to stand up for herself or her baby.

'Nothing serious, I hope,' Drakon said, looking concerned. 'No one sick?'

'No, no…' Kerry's voice trailed away as a barb of guilt twisted inside her—as if somehow by hiding his existence she was betraying her son. 'Personal things…nothing important.'

She took a breath and smiled reassuringly at the old man, who still looked worried—all the time feeling like the very worst kind of mother. How could she imply—even though of course she didn't really mean it—that giving birth to Lucas had not been important?

'I'm glad to hear that,' Drakon said, as he pushed his chair back and levered himself up to standing. Theo was on his feet beside him in an instant, but Drakon waved his help aside impatiently. 'I'm going to rest before dinner. Take a look around the house if you're interested. Tomorrow you can see the island.'

Kerry stood up too, and waited quietly as Theo held the door into the house open for their elderly host.

'The door stays open on its own,' Drakon said tartly as he shuffled past. 'I don't need your help.'

A smile flashed across Kerry's lips as she saw Drakon roll his eyes irritably at Theo. She really did like the old man.

Then she realised Theo was staring at her, and the smile faded from her face as quickly as it had come. A shiver prickled down between her shoulderblades as their eyes met—it felt just as if his dark gaze was boring right into her.

'Something amusing?' he asked, closing the distance between them in two long strides.

'I like Drakon,' she said, turning away to escape his penetrating gaze. 'It's good to see him again.'

She tried to concentrate on the amazing view of the bay below the house—a gorgeous crescent of rocky shoreline, edged by wizened old trees that seemed to lean right out over the azure Aegean Sea. But all the time she was ultra-aware of just how close Theo was standing.

Suddenly his arm slid possessively around her waist from behind, and she couldn't help drawing in a sharp breath. She tried to ignore the tremor that ran through her as his fingers brushed against her skin, just under the hem of her top.

'It's good to see *you* again,' he said, letting his hand slip further up inside, so that he was caressing the sensitive skin of her midriff.

'You're not looking at me,' Kerry said, attempting to pull away, but he held her firmly against him.

'Then it's good to *touch* you.' He eased her closer, so that she was standing with her back pressed against his chest.

'Touching me wasn't part of the deal,' she protested, instinctively pulling in her stomach muscles as his other hand slipped around her waist on the opposite side.

'We never made any deal.' His voice was a murmur, so close to her neck that his lips brushed her skin and set off a whole new series of tremors within her. 'You came because I told you to. And because you wanted to.'

'No. I—' Kerry's voice caught in her throat as Theo pressed his open mouth against her neck and nibbled gently, making exquisite sensations ripple through her.

She couldn't hide the way her body was suddenly trembling. Maybe it was because it was so long since she had felt Theo's touch, but suddenly the combination of his tongue moving across her skin and his warm breath feathering her neck felt like the most sensual thing she had ever experienced.

Her breath escaped her in a long, shuddery sigh, and he responded immediately by rocking his hips forward and pressing against her. The feel of his hard erection nudging into the soft curve of her bottom made a torrent of hot arousal cascade through her and her heart started to race.

'I've missed this,' Theo said. 'And I can tell you've missed it too.'

'No. I haven't.' Kerry's voice faltered as Theo ran his tongue lightly up the side of her neck and pulled on her earlobe with his lips. Another wave of tremors rolled through her—but she knew she had to put a stop to Theo's seduction.

If she let herself fall any further under his spell she wouldn't stand a chance—she knew she would end up in his bed. She could not let that happen. Not after the way he had treated her. And not with the huge secret she was keeping from him.

'I want to have a look around,' she said, taking a positive step forward and breaking away from his touch. 'Drakon said we could. I'm surprised you don't seem keen to take the opportunity to survey your potential acquisition.'

A smile spread slowly across Theo's face as Kerry pulled away from him, and he released his grip, letting her slip out of his arms. He burned to make love to her—hot, hard, passionate love—but he would wait until tonight.

He knew how much she still wanted him—it had been impossible for her to hide the way he'd so easily set her body alight with desire. She might be playing hard to get, but that just made him want her even more.

He walked behind her as she headed for a gap in the trees at the edge of the paved area. The view of the shimmering sea stretching out from the bay beneath them was stunning, but he only had eyes for the sublime sway of Kerry's hips as she moved.

God, he'd missed her—missed losing himself in her beautiful, receptive body.

Theo would never forgive her for what she had done—she'd abused his trust to interfere with matters that did not concern her, and the consequences could have been tragic. She would never share his life again—but she would share his bed that night.

'Drakon doesn't like change.' Kerry turned back to speak, taking him by surprise. 'He doesn't believe in discarding old things on a whim—just to get something bigger, better or flashier.'

'He's not totally averse to progress,' Theo pointed out, pulling his thoughts back from erotic images of making love to Kerry. 'He has a nice new helipad, and travels to Athens by helicopter whenever the whim takes him.'

'I wonder where he plans to live after he sells the island,' she said.

Theo frowned. 'It's not going to be easy to persuade him. I think he'd like to end his days here. But he also wants to leave things in order for his daughter,' he said. 'She lives on the mainland with her family, but from what I understand she has her hands full looking after her husband, who was injured in an accident. She has no head for business and Drakon doesn't want to add to her burden.'

'He's a thoughtful man.' Kerry stopped and looked at him. Her silky-soft hair was blowing in the breeze coming off the sea and she put up her hand to hold her fringe out of her eyes. 'How do you know all that? I don't believe *he* told you. He seems to be quite a private person.'

'That's not your concern,' Theo said, lifting his hand to cover hers. Her fingers felt cool and slim beneath his. 'Why did you cut your hair?'

For a moment her eyes opened wide with surprise, and in the bright Greek sunlight Theo saw that they *were* the clear blue he had believed them to be—then she schooled her features into a blank expression and met his gaze steadily.

'I felt like a change,' she said. 'But now I'm growing the fringe out again—that's why it's always in my eyes.'

'I like to see your face.' He lifted his other hand and smoothed all the tendrils back from her forehead.

'You weren't there, so I didn't think you'd mind.' She shook her head with a touch of irritation and he let go.

Her hair fell forward again, but not before he'd noticed the horizontal creases that had appeared across her forehead when she frowned. 'I'm going inside to get changed for dinner,' she added, turning away and heading for the house.

'You go on ahead,' he said. 'I'm going to look round a bit more.'

He watched her walk across the paved area and into the house, the bewitching movements of her body sending another surge of hot desire through his veins.

Her body seemed different somehow—slightly fuller, perhaps. Maybe it was his imagination, because he was so hot for her, but her breasts definitely seemed bigger than he remembered them. He pictured the way they'd look naked in his mind's eye—gorgeously ripe and full—and suddenly it was almost more than he could do not to follow her straight to the bedroom.

There was time to make love before dinner, but he wanted to make love to her properly, till he was utterly spent and all the tension had been burned out of him. That would take longer. A lot longer.

Kerry could feel Theo's eyes burning a hole in her back all the way across the patio. It was a relief to enter the cool interior of the house, but she was wound far too tightly to relax properly.

She hurried straight to their room, then showered and changed for dinner as quickly as she could. She was ready far too early—but she didn't want Theo to come back before she was dressed. From the way he'd been looking at her she knew exactly what he wanted to do—and that was the last thing she wanted. Or so she told herself.

She paced uneasily around the room for a few minutes, then decided to go out again. At least that way she could avoid being trapped in a confined space with him. Chances were that he wouldn't come on too strongly if they could be interrupted at any moment.

She closed the door quietly, then made her way along the corridor, admiring the many paintings that were hung along the simple whitewashed walls. She realised they were all different views of the island, and they were all painted by the same artist. There seemed to be something familiar about them, but she couldn't pinpoint what it was.

She was still looking at the paintings when Theo returned. Her heart skipped a beat as he paused beside her, and she could feel the heat radiating off his powerful body, smell his warm, musky scent. He was slightly flushed and looked as if he'd been hurrying.

'It took me longer to climb back up the cliff path than I expected,' he said. 'Drakon is waiting for us in the dining room. Go and join him—I'll be there very soon.'

She watched him stride away to their room, feeling her heart rate slowly subside once he was out of sight. She was happy to go and talk to Drakon. It was safer than spending time with Theo. And she was interested in finding out something about the paintings she had been admiring.

It wasn't long before Theo joined them and dinner was served. The meal that followed began much more easily than Kerry had anticipated. For the most part Theo carried the conversation, keeping the topics light and undemanding. She found herself starting to relax. It was almost possible to imagine that this was an ordinary social event like the many events she had attended with Theo in the past. Actually, it was more pleasant than many—she liked Drakon and enjoyed hearing his views on the world.

Theo was a charming and attentive companion. His manner seemed so natural and so familiar—so much like the way he had always behaved towards her when they were together. In fact there was nothing to distinguish the way he was treating her now from the way he had treated her during the year she'd been his lover.

She knew that tonight it was just an act—that he was simply playing the role of devoted lover—but it reminded her painfully of the past. Then suddenly, out of the blue, she found herself wondering if he had always been acting with her.

If he could turn on the charm now—even though she knew for sure that his feelings towards her were the complete opposite of those he was portraying—how could she know he'd ever been genuine? Had he ever really cared—or had she been nothing more than a suitably undemanding, biddable candidate who was willing to travel with him, to be at his beck and call for his personal convenience?

That thought felt like a slap in the face.

This evening showed that he was a master of deception. There was no way of knowing if he had ever been true to her—if his affection had ever been anything more than an act.

She stared at him across the table, unable to keep her expression neutral. After everything—what was she doing here with him?

She thought about Lucas. It made her chest ache, she missed him so much. She'd never been away from him overnight. By now Bridget would already have put him down to sleep. Had he settled quickly? Or had he cried because he missed his mother?

'Kerry?' Theo's voice cut into her thoughts, and she realised he had spoken to her more than once before she'd heard. 'Our host is saying goodnight.'

She quickly turned to Drakon, noticing how tired and drawn he was looking.

'That was a delicious meal,' she said quickly, hoping he hadn't noticed how distracted she'd become towards the end.

'Don't have the stamina I once had,' Drakon muttered as he heaved himself up on unsteady legs.

'Let me help,' Kerry said, rushing over to support him.

'I don't mind accepting help from a pretty young woman,' he replied.

She could tell he was trying to make his voice sound light, but the strain that he was trying to hide was clearly visible in his face. She helped him halfway across the room, then his assistant appeared with a wheelchair, which he gratefully sank into.

'Didn't want you to see this,' he mumbled. 'Don't really need it, but...'

'Thank you for a lovely evening,' she said, bending down to kiss him lightly on the cheek before his assistant wheeled him away.

She straightened her shoulders, already feeling Theo's eyes on her. For a moment she didn't want to turn and face him—but there was nothing else she could do.

'Alone at last.'

Theo's deep voice oozed with intent, and the sexual message in his tone tingled down her spine like a dark promise.

Kerry's feet felt as if they were glued to the floor, but she made herself turn on the spot until she was facing Theo. Their eyes met with a snap, and she felt a surge of emotion rush through her. It had been so easy for him to play the attentive lover that evening—but she *knew* he was just playing a role for the sake of their elderly host. Had it been that way all the time they were together?

'Was it always just an act?' she demanded.

CHAPTER FIVE

A GLIMMER of surprise flashed across Theo's face, but it was gone in an instant, to be replaced by a hard, shuttered expression. It was clear that he didn't intend to get into the discussion that she wanted—at least not in Drakon's dining room.

'I'm not sure I understand your meaning.' His voice sounded smooth and unhurried, but he closed the distance between them with a few rapid strides and wrapped his arm snugly around her. Although to an onlooker the gesture might have appeared affectionate, Kerry knew that was far from the truth. 'Let's go to our room, where we can talk quietly.'

'You know exactly what I mean,' she said curtly, attempting to pull away from him. But he tightened his hold on her and started walking out of the dining room. She had no choice but to go with him—not if she didn't wish to make a scene.

Reluctantly, she let him guide her back to their bedroom, clamped to his side by his powerful arm. She was acutely conscious of his firm, masculine body moving beside her. With every step they took she could feel his legs brushing against hers, feel his muscles working, feel the heat passing from his body to hers. It was as if there was a current flowing from him into her, making her more and more sensitive to him.

Her pulse-rate was rising and she was starting to feel slightly breathless. But it wasn't because of the strong emotions that had flared within her. Something else was building inside her now.

She tried desperately to ignore the way she was feeling physically—to call back the anger that had sparked in the dining room. But her mind and emotions were clouded simply from being so close to Theo.

'Let's not talk,' he said as he closed the door quietly behind them. He turned and pulled her towards him, face to face. 'I can think of things I'd far rather be doing with you.'

'No.' Kerry lifted her hands and pressed her palms flat against his chest to hold him away from her, although he was drawing her closer and closer with every second that passed. 'I want answers. I want to know if everything was always just an act. Did you never care for me at all?'

'An act?' Theo looked deep into her eyes in a way that sent a quiver of heat running right to her centre. 'You know this isn't an act. No one could fake sexual chemistry like this.'

'I'm not talking about the chemistry,' Kerry protested, trying not to be distracted by the heat of his chest through the fine fabric of his shirt. Her fingers twitched, longing to delve inside his clothing and feel his naked skin. 'There was more than that between—'

She hadn't finished speaking when Theo's mouth came down on hers, silencing her with a kiss. She gasped in surprise and he pushed his advantage home, plunging his tongue between her open lips.

It was a forceful possession of her mouth that she hadn't consciously invited—but her response was instant. An immediate rush of excitement tore through her body, making her tremble and moan with desire. It was as if her ability to resist him had evaporated in an explosion of pure physical arousal, and she arched towards him, moulding herself to his body.

His hands slid over her, touching and stroking through her dress. His tongue writhed erotically against hers, sending her pulse-rate soaring and making her head spin. It was impossible to think. Impossible to do anything other than surrender to Theo and kiss him back with equal passion.

Then, through the hot haze of sexual desire, she felt his hands moving on her hips. He was tugging at her dress, bunching the fabric up so that he could reach underneath.

A blast of feverish anticipation shot through her, making her legs buckle simply at the thought of what might happen next—of what she was suddenly desperate to experience again.

Theo's arms went around her, lifting her on to the bed, and for a moment she lay back breathlessly against the pillows, staring up into his flushed face. He was leaning over her, his black hair falling forward over his brow, filling her vision, blocking out everything but him.

His hand was on her leg, sliding quickly past her knee, along the inside of her thigh. Her whole being yearned for him, wanted to be one with him again.

But it would never happen—not truly. Not in the way her heart wanted.

He didn't love her. He'd never loved her.

'No.'

The word was hardly audible, but it was enough to make Theo stop completely still. His hand was resting just a few inches from the very top of her leg, right next to the most sensitive place on her body.

'Don't try to tell me you don't want this.' His tone was level, but Kerry could hear that he was breathing hard. She knew that he was fully aroused and expecting to make love to her.

'Not this,' she said, trying hard not to wriggle. The position of his hand was driving her to the point of distraction. If she rocked her hips it would move, slide intimately against her throbbing flesh. 'I want an answer to my question.'

'I told you—this is real,' he said, squeezing her inner thigh lightly. He didn't move his hand any higher, but the gentle pressure on her leg was enough to send waves of sensation rolling across the centre of her desire.

'Oh.' She couldn't help sighing in pleasure. She closed her eyes for a moment, drawing in a shaky breath.

'You want this,' Theo said. 'You want to make love.'

Kerry opened her eyes and looked at him.

'It's not love,' she said.

'No,' Theo replied, studying her through narrowed eyes. 'No one ever said it was.'

'But I thought that you had feelings for me,' Kerry said shakily, finally finding the will to push his hand away and sit up against the pillows. 'I thought that we had feelings for each other. At least that's how it seemed.'

'Feelings?'

Theo pulled away abruptly and stared at her in disgust. How dared she bring up the subject of their feelings?

She was the one who'd betrayed his trust—gone behind his back and stirred up trouble, almost causing a family tragedy.

'Don't even think of trying that one,' he bit out, standing up beside the bed. 'What kind of fool do you take me for? I can't be manipulated so easily.'

Her face was flushed and he could see the rapid rise and fall of her breasts as she breathed. She was just as turned on as he was—yet she was tormenting them both, trying to make him say something unguarded in the heat of passion.

He saw her shrink back a little, and her eyes widened with surprise, as if she was startled by his sudden change of temper. But then her expression hardened and her brow creased with annoyance. He knew she was about to challenge him.

'You have always been the one controlling our relationship. You still are—even though it's more than a year since you kicked me out,' she said, sliding off the opposite side of the bed and turning to face him. 'So don't talk to me about manipulation—I've always done everything you ever asked of me.'

'We *have* no relationship,' Theo grated. 'It ended the night you betrayed the trust I'd placed in you.'

He was shocked to hear her use the present tense— surely she knew the score as well as he did? This was just sex—nothing more. Why would she make it sound as if their affair was ongoing?

'You threw me out without a second thought,' she said. 'And now it suits your purpose you want me back.'

'I don't want you back,' he said through gritted teeth.

'But you still made me come here with you,' Kerry said. 'And you're deliberately messing with my head— acting like a devoted lover and trying to seduce me.'

'You understood the situation when you came here,' he said. 'So don't act surprised by the way I've treated you in public. And in private you want me just as much as you ever did.'

Kerry bit her lip and stared at Theo, feeling lost and utterly humiliated.

He was right. She did still want him. Despite everything, she *did* still want him.

'I never meant anything to you,' she said, hearing her voice crack with emotion. 'You've never even had the slightest respect for me.'

'Respect?' he repeated incredulously. 'After everything, how can you even *mention* respect?'

It was the confirmation she'd been dreading—proof

that she'd never meant anything to him at all. That was why it had been so easy for him to discard her when she did something foolish.

She felt her heart breaking all over again. Tears pricked her eyes, but she blinked them away, refusing to let him see her cry. He didn't respect her—but she had to show some respect for herself.

'Get away from me,' she said. 'I don't want to be in the same room as you.'

'I'm not leaving,' he said. 'I'm not asking our host for separate rooms. That would defeat the point of you being here.'

'Then I will,' Kerry said. She turned and stepped quickly towards the door.

Theo moved like lightning. In an instant he had circled the bed, and caught up with her just as she reached for the door handle.

His fingers closed like a vice around her wrist and he flipped her round, pinning her to the wall.

'Don't do something you'll regret.' His voice was deep and rough, as if he was only just holding his temper in check, and she could feel the tension in his muscular frame as he pushed up against her.

'It's too late for that,' she whispered miserably. 'I should never have come here with you in the first place.'

He pressed her back to wall with one hard thigh thrust between her legs and stared straight into her eyes. His gaze held her trapped as securely as the strength in his large, powerful body, and she could feel the angry energy emanating from him.

Then he released her with such abruptness that she stumbled forward into the room.

She was still finding her balance when she realised he had gone. He'd moved so quickly and shut the door so silently that it was almost as if he'd simply vanished.

She staggered over to the bed, breathing in jerky, painful gasps. Her eyes were swimming with tears, but she wouldn't let them fall. She would *not* let them fall. She could not let him win any more.

But she knew it wasn't over. No matter how many times she cried, or how hard she tried to hide the pain, it would never be over—because she was the mother of his son.

The following morning Kerry woke to the sound of the shower running in the *en suite* bathroom—Theo must have come back, but she had no idea when. It had taken her hours to fall asleep, but he hadn't disturbed her when he came into the room.

She frowned, wondering when he'd returned—and if he'd slept elsewhere and just come back to shower, or if he'd slipped into the bed during the night while she was sleeping.

She got up quickly, collected some fresh clothes from her case and sat at the table flicking through a magazine, intending to dash straight into the bathroom as soon as he appeared. After their argument she was not looking forward to the day, and she wanted to be washed and dressed before she had to talk to him again. She had the feeling he was going to make her pay for not meekly complying with his wishes the night before.

A minute later she heard the door to the bathroom open.

'Good morning.' Theo's voice seemed deeper than usual, and for a second Kerry wondered how much sleep he'd had—not much, if his gruff tone was anything to go by. But most importantly she realised his tone was neutral—he didn't sound angry any more. A ripple of relief ran through her and she turned to reply.

'Good morn…' She faltered, staring at him standing in the doorway—naked apart from a small white towel wrapped around his hips—and all coherent thought flew out of her head.

He looked absolutely magnificent, and she could not drag her eyes off him. His skin was still glistening with water droplets and his wet hair was sexily dishevelled, as if he'd just roughly towel-dried it.

He started walking towards her across the room, and she swallowed reflexively, simply staring at him in awe. The movement of his muscles rippling beneath his taut bronzed skin was totally mesmerising. And totally arousing.

Her gaze slid easily over the contours of his broad chest, down to the sculptured beauty of his lean stomach muscles. A sprinkling of black hair arrowed downwards, drawing her gaze lower still.

Her eyes widened as she found herself staring at his towel. Her attention was having a powerful effect on him, and he was making no attempt to hide it. She pressed her teeth into her lower lip, feeling an answering heat flood through her own veins.

She jumped up awkwardly, clutching the bundle of

fresh clothes to her chest, suddenly desperate to get out of there. She couldn't bear a repeat of last night's humiliation.

'There's no need for you to hurry,' Theo said, blocking her access to the *en suite* bathroom with his large, virtually naked body. 'Unfortunately Drakon cannot see us yet. We'll have to occupy ourselves for a while.'

'Oh,' she said, forcing herself to meet his gaze, but hardly registering his words as he lifted his hand to brush her hair back from her face. She knew exactly how he wanted to occupy himself—and, despite everything, her treacherous body felt the same way.

She shivered as his fingers made contact, knowing he was watching her reaction. She was certain he was aware how much she still wanted him—even after she had pushed him away the night before—but she would not give in to the desire that was rapidly taking her over.

She felt her cheeks flare even hotter and she stepped quickly to the side. His hand dropped slowly from her face, skimming lightly down the side of her body, but he didn't try to stop her as she fled into the bathroom.

When she emerged some time later she discovered that she was on her own again. A delicious breakfast had been laid out on their private balcony, but only one place had been set. She was to eat alone.

Like many Greeks, Theo rarely bothered with breakfast. Kerry felt light-headed if she skipped a meal—she couldn't imagine how Theo, six foot two inches of solid muscle, powered his body and made vital business decisions fuelled by nothing more than the occasional coffee.

She sat down, realising it was a welcome relief to be able to eat alone in the morning sunshine, enjoying the stunning view across the island to the Adriatic. The land sloped away from the house, down to olive groves shimmering silvery green, and beyond that the sea was a beautiful pale turquoise, wreathed with a slight sea mist that she knew would soon burn off as the day heated up.

She was just finishing her meal when Theo returned.

'I have some disappointing news,' he said, stepping out to join her on the balcony. 'Drakon is not well, and there is no chance we will be able to meet with him this morning. However, we do have his permission to walk up to the highest point on the island.'

'Oh, no—I hope it's nothing serious,' Kerry said.

'I don't know,' Theo said dispassionately, moving over to the edge of the balcony and leaning out to get a better view of the hill beside the house. 'His health is poor—which I believe is what prompted him to consider selling the island. Do you have suitable footwear? I'm not sure how rough the path will be.'

Kerry frowned, staring crossly at Theo's impassive expression. He didn't care at all that the poor old man was unwell—he just viewed it as a business opportunity.

'Give me a moment to change,' she said shortly, heading back inside without looking at Theo again.

'The island is small—only a few kilometres across—and there are no good roads or transport,' Theo said as they left the house. 'But we should be able to get a good view from the top of the hill.'

He watched Kerry step through the doorway ahead of him, letting his gaze run down her body appreciatively. She was wearing light cotton trousers that pulled snug over the gorgeous curves of her bottom as she walked, and a loose-fitting top that rippled against her in the slight breeze that was blowing in from the sea.

'Poor Drakon,' she said, as if the sight of the table under the trees where the old man had entertained them had suddenly made her think of him. 'I hope he feels better soon.'

'I know his staff are taking good care of him,' Theo replied.

He glanced down at the paving stones, noticing for the first time that the drifts of dead leaves and old olive blossom had been swept up. A wry smile flashed momentarily across his face as he realised it had been done for Kerry's benefit, but not for *his* initial visit, when he'd been on his own.

It was interesting that Drakon had made a concession to his inflexible 'take me as I am' persona for Kerry's sake. The old man really liked her, and Theo knew that bringing her here had been a wise move. Her presence had brought him one step closer to fulfilling his mother's dying wish.

They left the house and headed up the hill through olive groves that seemed almost as ancient as the land itself. It wasn't long before they were out from the shelter of the trees and looking at the final steep climb to the top of the hill.

'Do you want to rest for a moment?' Theo turned to look at Kerry and spoke for the first time since they'd left the house. His tone was neutral, but somehow Kerry got the feeling he didn't want her to take him up on his offer of rest.

'No, I'm fine,' she said quickly. She felt uneasy at the thought of sitting still with Theo anyway—especially as it was clear that he was keen to keep moving.

The silence between them was deafening, but all the time they were walking the atmosphere had been tolerable. Concentrating on keeping her footing and admiring the stunning scenery had distracted her from Theo's taciturn brooding.

He looked straight ahead and kept on walking without breaking his stride. It was still a fair hike to reach the top of the hill, and from the way Kerry's muscles were already aching it felt more like a mountain.

By the time they reached the summit she was breathing heavily, and her legs felt like jelly. She sat down on a large boulder to catch her breath, and gazed at the beautiful scenery. The mist had cleared to reveal an amazing view of the nearest neighbouring island. It was many times larger than Drakon's island, and he had told her that it had a reasonable population for its size.

'When you've rested for a moment we'll head back down,' Theo said, staring out across the glittering sea.

'We only just got here!' she gasped in surprise. 'Don't you want to look around or something?'

'I've seen all I need to see—and in any case nothing will alter my intention to buy the island.' Theo turned to look down at her and a flash of surprise showed on his face as he registered how heavily she was breathing. 'Now I want to get back, in case Drakon feels well enough to see us. I don't intend to miss an opportunity to move my negotiations with him forward.'

'He's sick!' Kerry exclaimed. 'Can't you leave him in peace?'

'I wouldn't dream of disturbing his peace.' Theo studied her through narrowed eyes. 'But this is business—and Drakon is looking for a buyer. Are you ready to get going?'

Kerry stared up at him crossly. She'd barely caught her breath, and her muscles were still burning from the effort of climbing the steep hill—but Theo hadn't even really needed to come up here!

She might have felt differently if they'd climbed slowly, enjoying the sunshine and the scenery, possibly even chatted a bit. But he'd just marched her up to the top of the hill in stony silence, to prove something to Drakon—perhaps to show that his interest in the island was genuine. Or maybe that he appreciated the privilege the old man had granted him when he'd allowed him to roam unaccompanied on his land.

Whatever his reasons, he had shown Kerry very little consideration—he'd been driven purely by his own agenda. Suddenly their conversation from the previous day, when they'd first arrived on the island, flashed into her mind. Even back when she'd thought he cared about her Theo really had done everything for his own personal convenience.

'If you always knew I got travel sick, why did you never say anything about it?' she demanded.

'I didn't think you wanted me to,' Theo replied, without missing a beat, although her comment must have seemed completely out of the blue. 'I thought you preferred not to think about it too much.'

She paused, staring at him through narrowed eyes. In a way he was right—she did try not to dwell on it. And any distraction, apart from reading, was usually a good way to feel better. But that didn't excuse him for never showing her any concern.

'How did you even know I didn't feel well?' she asked.

'It seemed fairly obvious—to me at least,' he replied. 'You went pale and shaky. And very quiet. But you usually seemed to recover pretty quickly once you were back on firm ground.'

'If you knew how I felt why did you make me travel so much?' she asked accusingly.

'I assumed you didn't want to let it interfere with your life,' he said. 'You never liked admitting any weakness. Like just now—apparently the climb was too much for you, but you haven't said anything.'

'It wasn't too much for me,' she said, infuriated by his patronising tone. 'Come on. Let's get going again.'

She sprang up to her feet, but her legs still felt like jelly. For a moment she wobbled slightly, and he was beside her in an instant, wrapping his arm around her waist.

'Your legs are shaking.' His voice was suddenly deep

and sensually loaded. 'But—as you insist the climb wasn't too much for you—maybe it's me making you tremble.' He hugged her tightly to him with one arm and lifted his other hand to brush her hair off her face. 'In fact I can remember many different ways I used to make you tremble and shake.'

'Let go of me!' Kerry snapped, despite the fire that suddenly burned through her veins at the images he conjured in her mind. 'I don't want you to touch me again. Not ever.'

'Really? I don't think that is completely honest.' Theo stepped away from her. 'But it seems that honesty was never a central part of our relationship.'

'I was always honest with you,' she said defensively.

'Maybe you never lied to me directly,' Theo said. 'But you lied by omission. Neither of us discussed your travel sickness—but we both knew about it.'

'And what does *that* say about our relationship?' Kerry asked, thinking that they'd never really talked about anything important.

'I hardly think *that* was the defining point of our relationship,' Theo said derisively. 'Another moment stands out far more clearly in my memory—the moment you went behind my back and betrayed me.'

'No. It wasn't meant like that,' Kerry replied automatically, but as the words left her mouth she knew the past didn't matter. Whatever had happened between them in the past was completely irrelevant.

She was guilty of dishonesty now.

She was keeping his son a secret.

A wave of emotion washed over her, squeezing her heart and making her throat tight. Baby Lucas was thousands of miles away, being looked after by someone else, and she was here, with Theo, and the secret she was keeping seemed to be growing more awful with every passing minute.

CHAPTER SIX

THEO started striding down the steep path back towards the house. Kerry followed behind, struggling to keep up. He was a very tall, athletic man, with a lengthy stride, and it seemed his bad temper was making him walk even faster than normal.

It was typical arrogant behaviour, she thought bitterly. He was making no concession to her naturally slower pace, but there was no way she was going to ask him to slow down. Her legs were still shaky, but so was the whole of her body—inside and out. She flicked her fringe back from her damp forehead and kept walking.

All she could think about was Lucas.

She'd kept him secret because she was scared of what might happen—of what Theo might do. She'd seen for herself that he'd been so protective of his brother's son that he'd wanted to take him away from Hallie.

Kerry had not been able to stand by and watch that happen. For personal reasons she couldn't bear to see a child forcibly taken from its mother. But her own background had also taught her that lies and deception led to heartache and tragedy—and by keeping Lucas a secret she was guilty of that herself.

Without warning her eyes blurred with tears. She wanted to do what was right for everyone—but she was too scared of the possible consequences if she told Theo.

Suddenly her foot hit a rut, and she staggered forward on the steep path, letting out a sharp cry of alarm.

Theo shot back up the slope and was beside her almost before she'd realised that she was lying headlong on the ground, her face pressed against the loose dirt path, pebbles digging into the palms of her hands.

'Kerry? Are you all right?' His deep voice sounded genuinely troubled, and for a moment she was startled by how familiar it sounded.

Only a moment ago she'd been convinced Theo had never shown any concern for her—but now she realised she'd been mistaken. The tender tone of his voice was achingly familiar, and made fresh tears swim in her eyes.

'Are you injured?' he asked, his hand gently cupping her shoulder.

'No—I'm fine.' She pushed her hands against the path to lever herself up, but it was hard with her head down and the stones jabbing into her palms.

Theo reached for her immediately, helping her into a sitting position, and stared into her face. His expression was so intense that for a moment she was glad she was wearing her sunglasses. She didn't want him to see her tear-filled eyes.

'My legs were wobbly,' she said, feeling her cheeks flare at the thought of how she'd been sprawled so humiliatingly on the ground in front of him. 'I'm not used to climbing up mountains.'

'Then you should have asked for a longer break,' he said sharply. 'It's not responsible to push yourself too hard out here—you know how isolated we are.'

She gasped, stung by his harsh tone of voice.

'You just want to avoid the expense of calling a helicopter if I sprain my ankle,' she retorted. She hadn't been deliberately careless—*he* was the one who'd been walking so fast.

'If you're foolish enough to sprain your ankle I'll carry you back myself,' he said. 'Over my shoulder,' he added, letting his eyes run across her as if he was assessing how easy she would be to carry.

Kerry glared at Theo, suddenly furious with him for being so heartless. What if she really hadn't been fit enough to keep up with him? She hadn't exactly had much time to keep herself in shape lately. Looking after Lucas and working in the travel agency took up every minute of her time. She wasn't Theo's adoring lover any more— with nothing better to do than run around after him.

'Thankfully, that won't be necessary,' she said coldly, ignoring the flush of embarrassment that heated her face at the thought of being carried over his shoulder. 'Let's get going—I thought you were keen to get back.'

Theo studied her from beneath dark brows as she pushed herself up to her feet—she was still a little unsteady, but she looked all right.

'We'll go a little slower on the way down,' he said. 'But first you need to wipe your face—it's covered with dirt.'

Kerry drew in a startled breath and rubbed her fingers across her face.

'Lucky for me you are trying to impress Drakon,' she said, looking down at her dirt-streaked fingertips before lifting her eyes to meet his gaze straight on. 'Or you might never have bothered to tell me I've got half the path stuck to my face.'

The rest of the day passed slowly for Kerry. They'd arrived back at Drakon's house before lunch, but he'd still not been feeling well enough to receive visitors, so Theo had spent the afternoon working on his laptop, and Kerry had sat in the shade of the wizened old olive trees on the paved area, trying to read.

It was a wonderful place to sit, but despite her lovely surroundings she found it impossible to relax. She kept thinking about Lucas, and questioning whether she was making a terrible mistake.

It was one thing to hide her pregnancy and then her child from Theo when he was in another country—after all, at the time she'd had very good reasons for keeping her secret. But now that she was back in Greece with Theo everything seemed different.

That morning, when he'd accused her of dishonesty, his comment had cut her deeply—because she knew he was right. She wasn't being honest with anyone. Not with Theo. And most importantly not with Lucas.

She knew from personal experience just how devastating it was to discover that everything you believed to be true was actually false. Deception ruined lives—and she could not let her son's life be blighted by secrets and dishonesty.

By the time she went inside to get ready for dinner she had made an enormous decision. She would tell Theo about Lucas. She knew that he would want to be part of his son's life—but she also knew that she would *never* let him take Lucas away from her.

She wasn't like Hallie. Theo had told Corban that Hallie was not fit to be a mother, but Kerry would never give him reason to doubt her devotion and suitability as a mother. It was her right to take care of her son, and no one could take that away from her. But she *was* prepared to make changes. She would move to Athens, find a job and somewhere to live. Then Theo could have regular access to his son.

'Drakon is still too ill to join us for dinner,' Theo said, knocking her out of her thoughts as he came into their room.

'I do hope he will be okay,' Kerry said, worried about the old man again.

'The doctor is due to visit tomorrow,' Theo said. 'Meanwhile, we will be eating alone tonight. Why don't you shower first? I still have a few calls to make.'

'All right.' Kerry picked up a change of clothes and headed into the *en suite* bathroom. It was strangely familiar—getting ready for dinner first while Theo talked on his phone. She showered and dressed, and was just about to come out of the bathroom when Theo knocked sharply on the door.

'Kerry! Are you nearly done?'

'I'm here,' she said, opening the door. 'What is it?'
Somehow the urgency of Theo's voice had sent an icy
chill down her spine.

'Your sister, Bridget, called,' he said. 'I answered
your mobile because she was calling repeatedly and I
thought it might be important.'

'What is it?' Kerry's heart lurched with fear and her
throat closed with panic.

Oh, God—don't let it be Lucas! Don't let something
bad have happened to Lucas!

'Lucas has fallen,' Theo said. 'Down the stairs, I
think. Your sister sounded pretty upset. I think it best if
you go to her.'

'Oh, my God!' Kerry clamped her hand over her
mouth and slumped back against the doorframe in an
agony of distress.

All coherent thought flew out of her mind. All she
could do was imagine her poor, sweet baby boy falling
down the stairs.

Oh, God—she should never have left him. It was all
her fault. Lucas had come to harm and she wasn't there
with him. She would never forgive herself—she should
never have left him.

Theo stared at her, momentarily shocked at the
strength of her reaction to the news about her nephew.
She had gone as white as a sheet, and she was shaking
so violently that he could see it from across the room.
He swore under his breath in Greek, cursing himself for
not breaking the news to her gently.

'I think it's all right,' he said, taking hold of her

upper arms and shaking her slightly to get her to look at him. 'They've taken him to the hospital—but they think he's okay.'

'He's only six months old.'

She stared up him, her eyes drowning in tears, and he wasn't entirely sure she'd understood what he'd said. His chest contracted as he saw her distress, and he knew he had to find a way to comfort her.

'A helicopter is on the way,' he told her. 'And my jet is waiting in Athens to take us to London.'

'You're taking me there?' she asked, as if she was finally starting to come out of her state of shock.

'Yes. I'll come with you.' Theo guided her across the room to a chair and gently pushed her down into it. He could tell it would be pointless to try to make her eat or drink anything—hopefully she'd be able to have something on the plane. He knew that travelling on an empty stomach was the worst thing possible for her. And she'd need to be in a fit state to help her sister when they reached London.

He moved around the room swiftly, collecting up their belongings and packing them into small cases. It wouldn't be long before the helicopter was here.

Kerry sat in Theo's private plane, staring out of the window at the inky black night. Lucas should be tucked up in his own cot by now, with her to watch over him, not waiting to be seen by a doctor in a strange accident and emergency department—if that was where he even was. She didn't actually know for sure.

She'd made a frantic phone call before they'd left Athens, but Steve, Bridget's partner, hadn't heard anything. Mobile phones weren't allowed in hospital, and he was at home with their children, waiting for his mother to come and babysit. Then he would join Bridget at the hospital. When he knew anything—anything at all—he would call Kerry.

'We'll be there soon,' Theo said, coming to sit beside her. He smelled freshly showered, and when she glanced at him she saw his black hair was still damp. 'I have a car waiting for us at the airport.'

'Thank you,' Kerry said. 'It would have been a nightmare trying to get home by regular transport.'

'How are you feeling?' Theo asked, glancing at the half-eaten sandwich on the table in front of her.

'All right,' she lied, feeling her stomach roll over with nausea—but whether it was travel sickness or fear for Lucas she couldn't say.

'I'll get you some more iced water,' Theo said, standing up and going to fetch it from the bar himself.

Kerry watched him, realising that he'd done that for her a hundred times before when they were travelling. He'd always shown her little kindnesses—but in her distress over the brutal way he had ended their relationship she had blotted out so many of the good things.

'Lucas will be all right,' he said as he sat beside her once more. 'If it was bad news I'm sure Steve would've heard something.'

'Thank you for being so kind,' Kerry said.

'Family is everything,' he replied, his voice full of

genuine feeling. 'You know how much my own nephew means to me. Of course you feel the same about yours.'

Kerry drew her lower lip into her mouth and turned to look at him. She'd guessed he'd made the assumption that Lucas was Bridget's baby. She didn't know what her sister had told him—but from what Theo had said she'd been pretty upset. It would be natural for him to think that.

If she was ever going to confess her secret to him, then the moment was here.

'Lucas is not my nephew.' Her voice was quiet, but her heart was beating so loudly it almost deafened her. 'He is my son.'

'What?'

Theo stared at her in shock—not sure he had heard her correctly.

'Lucas is my son,' Kerry repeated.

She looked pale and sick, but she was meeting his gaze straight on—and he knew she was utterly serious. Then, almost as if his mind was working in slow motion, his thoughts pulled together to reach another obvious conclusion.

Kerry had said that Lucas was six months old. That meant six months…plus nine months…

'He is *my* son.'

The words sliced through the air like a knife—like a giant blade slicing through the reality of Theo's tightly disciplined and controlled world.

He had a son.

How could that be true? It didn't seem possible that such a monumental fact could have been kept hidden from him. Kerry had kept his son—his own flesh and blood—a secret from him.

Why hadn't she told him? The question flashed through his mind, but then he pushed it aside. *Why* didn't matter.

'You will regret this.'

'Having your son?' Her voice was thin and tremulous, as if she could sense the anger that was starting to build within him after the initial shock had sunk in.

'The fact that you kept him from me,' he said.

He stared at her pale face, feeling the violent thud of his heart beneath his ribs and the escalating fury surging around his body.

He had a son. He was a father. And Kerry had tried to stop him from knowing about it.

If it hadn't been for Drakon Notara's island Theo would never have gone looking for Kerry, and he would never have found out that he was a father. Even after they'd been together for more than a day it had taken this emergency for Kerry to confess to her deception. And that was probably because she knew she wouldn't be able to keep up the pretence at the hospital.

'You will not keep my son from me any longer.'

His voice throbbed with dangerous intent and his dark eyes bored into her like a weapon. Then he turned and walked away.

Kerry stared after him, shaking so hard that she had to grip on to the armrests. She knew trouble was coming.

Theo did not speak to her again apart from to confirm the details of which hospital Lucas had been taken to.

They sat in his limousine silently. Kerry was dimly aware of the tension simmering within him, but mostly she was overwhelmed with anxiety about Lucas.

They arrived at the hospital and she spotted Bridget and Steve almost immediately. They were waiting for her in the hospital entrance hall with baby Lucas. The doctors had already discharged him.

'Oh, my little one,' Kerry said, holding her baby tightly to her. 'Oh, my little angel.'

Her lips were trembling and her throat felt tight—then suddenly she burst into tears. Bridget was there with her, her arms around both of them.

'He's all right,' Bridget said, hugging her reassuringly. 'They said he's all right. I overreacted when he fell—but I just felt so terrible.'

Kerry looked down at her baby through a film of tears. His bright blue eyes fixed on her just as sharply as ever, and then he broke out into one of his most engaging smiles, with dimples dancing in his cute little cheeks.

Her eyes blurred once again as fresh tears formed, and all she could see was his thick black curly hair. Then she heard him giggle, and her relief and joy at their reunion was complete.

She blinked away her tears and held him tight—determined never to let him out of her sight again.

Theo stood to the side, watching events unfold through narrowed eyes. He understood that everything was all right. That Lucas was safe and sound. Lucas—his baby son—was safe and sound.

Kerry was crying and hugging the baby, and suddenly

Theo caught a glimpse of curly black hair as she turned slightly to the side. His son had curly black hair. Somehow that detail surprised him. In the couple of hours since he'd discovered he was a father he had never even wondered what his baby looked like. All babies looked alike, didn't they?

Suddenly he wanted to see his son properly, and he took a step closer. At that moment he heard a sound he couldn't immediately recognise. Then he realised what it was—Lucas was giggling.

It was a beautiful, pure sound—the sound of his baby son's happiness at being back in his mother's arms. Something inside Theo contracted. That was *his* baby. And no one was ever going to deprive him of even one more moment of his son's life.

The next few minutes passed for Kerry in a daze of overwhelming relief while Bridget tried to explain everything that had happened. But all Kerry could focus on was the fact that Lucas was all right. Apart from a few bruises he had survived his fall intact. It wasn't as bad as Bridget—in her state of guilty panic—had originally made it sound.

Kerry had imagined him falling from top to bottom of a flight of stairs, when in fact he had just tumbled down the short flight of steps that led from Bridget's kitchen to her utility room. Lucas wasn't crawling yet, but he could roll, and she had only turned her back for a second.

Theo had barely spoken. He had been perfectly polite to everyone at the hospital, but Kerry knew him well enough to know something was going on behind those dark, assessing eyes.

'Thank you for bringing Kerry so quickly,' Bridget suddenly gushed, throwing her arms around him and hugging him tightly.

'You are welcome,' he said, standing as still and un-yielding as a rock until she stepped back awkwardly. 'Thank *you* for contacting us earlier this evening,' Theo continued. 'I want you to know that I appreciate all you have done for Lucas—but now you and Steve should leave us and return home to your own children.'

'I…' Bridget paused, and looked at Kerry in confusion.

'He knows,' Kerry managed to say.

'Yes. I know that Lucas is my son,' Theo said. 'And now that I know I will take my responsibility as his father seriously.'

'What do you mean?' Bridget asked, looking wor-riedly from Kerry to Theo to Lucas, who was now dozing peacefully in Kerry's arms.

'I mean that from this point onwards I will take charge of his care,' Theo said.

'Hang on a minute,' Bridget said, rising to her sister's defence. 'You chucked Kerry out. You're the one who finished it—you didn't want to know her.'

'That was before I knew about my son,' Theo said. 'Everything is different now.'

'But you can't just waltz in here and—'

'It's all right, Bridget,' Kerry said. She knew Bridget was trying to protect her, and Kerry loved her sister dearly for it. Bridget was just a few years older than her—not old enough to have been involved in the conspiracy to keep Kerry in the dark about her mother. 'You go home now. This is something Theo and I have to sort out.'

'But—'

'Come on, love. You heard her,' said Steve, looking exhausted.

Kerry tried to smile at her sister reassuringly as Steve led her away. Inside she was a horrible mess of churning emotions, but at least she had Lucas back in her arms again. She bent forward and brushed her cheek against his soft curls, feeling a wave of love for her baby son. Lucas was all that mattered. And as long as she had him everything would be all right.

'We will go to a hotel for what remains of the night,' Theo said. 'Then tomorrow we will discuss the future.'

They travelled in the limousine in silence once more. But this time Lucas was secured in his car seat next to Kerry. The atmosphere between them had changed somehow—and not for the better.

Earlier she'd known Theo was furious with her, and she'd understood why. Even though his temper had been building, and sometimes he had seemed on the verge of exploding, she'd felt as if she'd known where she stood with him.

Now everything seemed different. She had no idea what he was feeling or thinking, because his expression had become as cold and impenetrable as ice.

She looked up and found him studying her. His eyes glinted in the dark. They bored into her like lucid black ice—freezing the blood in her veins and delivering a dreadful premonition of the storm that was brewing.

She shivered and looked away. She knew the freezing-cold fury that Theo was holding battened down under tight control was just as lethal as anything he'd been feeling earlier.

The limousine pulled up by the grand entrance of a top London hotel, and Kerry unfastened Lucas from his safety belt. She carried him inside and they were shown immediately up to a massive luxury suite. But if she'd expected separate rooms she'd been mistaken, because Theo insisted they all share one room.

'We are a family now,' he said, as he oversaw the arrival of a cot for Lucas. 'Because of his fall we will have our son in our room with us for a few days. Then he will have his own room.'

Theo's words sent a prickle of warning running down Kerry's spine—but she was totally exhausted and not entirely sure that she had heard him correctly when he'd said *our room*.

She bent over the cot to lay Lucas carefully inside, and as she straightened up she felt every muscle in her aching body protest. The last couple of days had been tough—physically and emotionally. And the last few hours had been overwhelming. She'd known that telling Theo about Lucas would change things—but even so she wasn't prepared for what happened next.

'In our room with us?' she repeated, feeling a shiver of anxiety as she straightened her shoulders and turned to face him. 'I don't understand what you are saying.'

'We are a family now,' Theo repeated.

Kerry drew in a shaky breath and lifted her eyes to meet his gaze. It was as hard and impenetrable as ever—but Kerry knew he meant business. A frozen wedge of ice settled in her stomach, and suddenly she was dreading what he would say next.

'Let me make myself clear,' Theo said. 'We will be married immediately.'

CHAPTER SEVEN

'MARRIED? You want me to marry you?' Kerry gasped.

This time she knew what Theo had said—she just couldn't believe it. After everything that had happened, how could he want to *marry* her? And why would he assume that she would accept?

'No—it's not what I *want*,' Theo said. 'But the situation has forced my hand.'

'I'm not *forcing* you to marry me,' Kerry said in shock, staring at him with wide eyes. He was making it sound as if she had done this deliberately—had his baby to coerce him in some way. 'It's not what I want either!'

'That much is clear,' Theo said flatly. 'Considering you took my son and hid him from me.'

'Then why are you telling me this?' Kerry said, raking her hands through her hair in frustration as the long fringe kept falling in her eyes.

'Because it is what's best for my son,' Theo said, walking across the room and looking down at the baby where he was lying in the cot. He was awake—looking sleepily at the lights moving across the ceiling from the city outside.

'*Our* son,' Kerry said automatically, feeling a shiver of foreboding as she saw just how intensely Theo was staring at Lucas. Already he seemed as possessively protective of him as he'd been of his nephew, Nicco. 'How is it best for our son to be brought up in a loveless marriage?'

'What do *you* think is best for him?' Theo asked harshly. 'To live in poverty in an inner-city studio flat, being looked after by strangers while his mother works?'

'It's not as bad as you make it sound,' Kerry said defensively, not even wondering how Theo knew exactly what kind of flat she lived in. 'I'm still getting myself back on my feet. Soon I'll be able to move—then he can have his own room.'

'*Then* he can have his own room?' Theo bit out incredulously. 'Stop being ridiculous. Now that I know I have a son he will never live like that—but that is not what's important.'

'You're right—material things don't matter,' Kerry said, hating the way Theo was tying her up in knots. 'I love him—that's all that matters. That's all he needs.'

'He needs his father,' Theo grated.

Kerry bit her lip and looked up at him. His eyes were narrowed dangerously, and he was staring at her with an expression of pure dislike. It cut her to the core. She'd never meant any of this to happen the way it had—but when he'd thrown her out she hadn't felt she had a choice. She'd been so scared that he would take her baby—just as he'd told his brother to take Nicco from Hallie.

'I'll move to Athens. Find a job.' Her voice was quiet but she managed to keep it steady—to show him she was serious about meeting him halfway. 'You can see him whenever you want. You can be part of his life.'

'This isn't a discussion,' Theo said coldly. 'We're not doing a deal here. I have told you that we will be married. That is the only option open to you.'

'I can't marry you,' Kerry said. 'You don't love me. It would be a sham. How would that be good for Lucas?' *Or for her*, a little voice inside her wept.

'Let me make it simple for you.' Theo took a step closer, so that he was looming over her. 'I realise I don't know much about your background—about the way you were brought up. But obviously you are close to Bridget, so you understand *something* about the importance of family.'

'Don't patronise me,' Kerry said, horrified that he was referring to her past. As far as she was aware he knew nothing about the awful truth of her upbringing. 'My past isn't relevant.'

'It is if you don't understand the importance of a father in a child's life,' Theo said. 'My son will not grow up under a different roof from his father. He will always know that I love him unequivocally and unconditionally. He will never, ever doubt my love for a single second of his life.'

Kerry stared up at him, feeling the passion in his voice rumbling through to her very soul. She knew that

Take a look at what's on offer at

www.millsandboon.co.uk

MILLS & BOON®
Pure reading pleasure

My Account / Offer of the Month / Our Authors / Book Club / Contact us

All of the latest books are there PLUS

- Free Online reads
- **Exclusive** offers and competitions
- At least **15% discount** on our huge back list
- Sign up to our **free** monthly eNewsletter

- More info on your favourite authors
- **Browse the Book** to try before you buy
- eBooks available for most titles
- Join the M&B community and **discuss** your favourite books with other readers

Search Countries I Affiliates I Site Map I Company Information I Careers I Privacy Policy Terms and Conditions I Aspiring Authors I Submit Manuscript I FAQs
Copyright © 2000 - 2008 Harlequin Mills & Boon Limited* All rights reserved.

Take a look at what's on offer at

www.milsandboon.co.uk

he meant every word that he said. He'd only known his son for an hour but already his love for him was burning brightly, shining out like a beacon.

Out of nowhere she felt tears welling in her eyes, and she turned away so that Theo wouldn't see them. How could she deny her son such powerful love?

She didn't even know who *her* father was. She had never felt love as all-encompassing as the love Theo was expressing for her son. How could she deny Lucas that?

'Lucas needs both his mother and his father,' Theo said. 'Despite the fact that you have tried to keep me out of his life, I can see how much you love him. I love him too, and want what's best for him. That means we must marry.'

Kerry blinked to clear her eyes, then turned back to face Theo.

'All right,' she said. 'I will marry you.'

The following day they flew back to Greece. Theo took them to the family's private island residence, saying that the peaceful isolation would be ideal for father and son to get to know each other.

Kerry could see the benefit of staying somewhere quiet, because Theo was always busy when they were staying in one of his many hotels. But it would mean that he was free to spend every minute with them, making it impossible for her to relax and let down her guard.

The only respite for Kerry that day was the time he spent on the telephone, enquiring after Drakon's health. He was still determined to acquire the old man's island,

and did not intend to let the slightest window of opportunity pass him by.

The next day, despite his good intentions to spend time with Lucas, Theo found he had to return to Athens on business. Kerry was secretly pleased. As she watched the helicopter take off she felt the knot of tension in her stomach start to ease. They'd spent most of the previous day travelling, and she was exhausted. And on top of that the atmosphere between them had become increasingly strained, making her feel that more trouble was brewing.

It was a welcome relief to spend the day playing with Lucas on her own. In the afternoon she decided to take him swimming. The huge infinity pool, where Theo habitually pounded through length after length, seemed far too big for them. But there was a smaller, child-friendly pool, shaded by an awning on one side. It seemed much more suitable for splashing about in with the six-month-old.

Kerry looked at the choice of swimwear that the housekeeper, Sara, had laid out on the bed for her—there was nothing but bikinis. At home, when she took Lucas to the local pool, she always wore a one-piece costume, but she had forgotten to bring it. Pregnancy had taken its toll on her body, and she wasn't completely back to her previous shape. And, to make matters worse, the lower part of her stomach was covered with red stretch marks.

Being on her own, she hadn't thought about them much. She'd always been too busy taking care of Lucas or working. Now, even though Theo was away in Athens, she was reluctant to leave her stomach uncovered. But she didn't want Lucas to miss out, so she slipped on a bikini, wrapped a towel around herself and carried him outside.

The water was gorgeous—just the right temperature and crystal-clear.

'Do you like that?' She laughed as Lucas giggled and splashed while she walked around the pool, pulling him through the water. He was already kicking his legs strongly, and she had a feeling that he would grow up to be a powerful swimmer—like his father.

After a while she took him over to the wide shallow steps that led into the pool and set him down on the top step, up to his waist in water. She sat on the step below, holding him up so that he could play safely with the little boats and balls she had found.

She knew the toys must belong to Nicco, and that made her think about Hallie and Corban. She deeply regretted what had happened on her last night in Athens, and she was nervous about seeing them again. But as they were away, travelling around Europe, she wouldn't have to face them for some time.

'Here's the little boat,' she said, floating the toy Lucas was playing with back towards him. He squealed with delight and batted it again, making a big splash. 'It's blue,' she said. 'A blue boat.'

She found herself thinking about her decision to marry Theo. It was always there, in the back of her mind, and it had been weighing on her constantly.

She was worried that she was taking a risk—that their marriage might be part of Theo's plan to get Lucas away from her. Once he'd established himself firmly as Lucas's father, maybe he intended to cut her out of his life. She *knew* that he'd encouraged Corban to take Nicco away from Hallie.

But, from the impassioned way he'd talked about a child needing both his parents, she didn't truly think that he would do that to Lucas and her.

The situation with Hallie had been different. Theo had been concerned that she was not a fit mother. Even though in Kerry's eyes that didn't justify his intended actions, she could understand his motivation. It also meant that she knew that she must never give Theo any grounds to doubt her own ability as a mother.

Suddenly, the unmistakable sound of a helicopter caught her attention. She looked up and saw that it was leaving the island—she must have been so lost in her thoughts that she hadn't heard it arrive. Theo was back on the island.

'I managed to get away earlier than I expected.' His voice right behind her nearly made her jump out of her skin.

'Hello.' She twisted round and looked up at him. He loomed over her, dressed in a dark business suit, with dark sunglasses hiding his eyes. His hair was ruffled from the helicopter's downdraft, and he had loosened his tie, but he didn't look remotely approachable. In fact he looked even more steely than usual, and the knot of tension started to tighten inside her again.

'I'll change, then come and join you in the water,' he said.

'No!' Kerry's voice squeaked unnaturally high in response to Theo's words. The idea of being semi-naked with him in the pool sent a wave of panic through her. 'No—I mean, we're coming out now. Lucas is getting tired.'

Then, as soon as the words were out of her mouth, she remembered her stretch marks. She didn't want Theo to see them. They were unattractive, and she was already self-conscious of the way her body had changed after her pregnancy. She couldn't get out with him standing there—she'd left the only towel on the sun lounger a couple of metres away.

'Would you pass me that towel?' she asked, thinking that she could hold Lucas against her shoulder as she stood up and let the towel drape across his body and down past her stomach. She looked up at Theo expectantly—there was no reason he shouldn't do as she'd asked—but she got the impression that he wasn't really listening. The expression on his face seemed intense, but she had no idea what he was thinking or feeling. 'The towel?' she repeated hopefully.

Theo took off his sunglasses and looked at Kerry, sitting on the second step, with the water lapping gently at her waist. His eyes followed the alluring shape of her hips below the surface, ran along her long slender legs down to her feet. Then his gaze tracked back up, roaming instinctively over her top half. She was wearing a pale blue bikini, which looked good next to her creamy skin. It seemed like a lifetime since he'd seen so much of her naked body, and a familiar surge of arousal powered through him.

On Drakon's island he had thought that her breasts seemed fuller than he remembered, and now he could see that it was true. She was breathing quickly, and the rapid rise and fall of her chest made him want to reach down and slip his hands inside the pale blue cups of the bikini, caress her luscious breasts and tease her pert nipples. He'd done that many times before, and she had always responded by melting in his arms. In fact it had been very rare that they had swum together and not ended up making love.

But right now he knew that Kerry was *not* pleased to see him. His arrival had startled her, and he'd seen her body language become defensive. She'd been like that with him ever since they took Lucas from the hospital—in fact her standoffishness seemed to be getting more pronounced.

It bothered him. He didn't like coming into a room and seeing her whole body become tense and hunched inwards. Even though he knew that the changes in her behaviour were barely perceptible—that no one else would notice—it was an affront to his masculine dignity. She'd used to tremble like a kitten when he approached her, and look up at him with sultry eyes that had let him know just how much she desired him. It had made him feel as powerful as a lion—and he'd swept her up into his embrace knowing that she was burning for him to make love to her.

Now everything was different. On Drakon's island the chemistry between them had still been there, but

she'd held back—presumably because she'd been worried he might find out about Lucas. However, since he'd
brought her back to Greece the atmosphere between
them had been increasingly cold and difficult.

He knew that she didn't want to marry him. If she
had any feelings for him at all, or any desire to share
his life, she would not have kept Lucas a secret from
him. That knowledge was demeaning—like a vicious
slap round the face.

The sound of splashing and giggling pulled him out
of his thoughts. He looked down, letting his eyes skim
past Kerry to his baby son.

His bright blue eyes were twinkling merrily, his curly
black hair was glistening with water and he was splashing and chuckling energetically. To Theo's untutored
eyes he didn't seem all that tired, but he didn't know
much about babies. If Kerry said he was tired then he
probably was.

'Let me take him while you get out,' he said, putting his sunglasses into his pocket and reaching down
to the baby.

He closed his large hands around Lucas's warm little
body and lifted him straight up and out of the water.
Lucas gave a high-pitched squeal and Theo felt an
answering bolt of alarm shoot through him—he'd
moved too abruptly and frightened his son.

He held him up in front of his face and looked at him
worriedly. But then Lucas squealed again, and suddenly
Theo realised he wasn't crying. He was excited. He'd
enjoyed being flown straight up.

He found himself smiling as he gazed into his son's face, and as they made eye contact he felt an unexpected wave of emotion roll through him. This extraordinary little person was his son—his own flesh and blood.

Then, at that moment, he realised he was dangling Lucas in front of him in what seemed an entirely unnatural position. Perhaps he should wrap him in a towel and hold him against his shoulder. He had to do something—but suddenly he felt awkward, and didn't know how to manoeuvre the baby.

He turned to look at Kerry, but she was still sitting in the pool on the steps, hugging her knees up to her chest. Why wasn't she helping him? Was she trying to prove something by letting him struggle alone?

'Pass me that towel,' he said.

Kerry bit her lip and stared up at Theo. Seeing him hold her son—*their* son—for the first time made a strange feeling run through her. She'd seen an expression of love pass across Theo's face as he met his son's eyes, and it had filled her with an uncomfortable mixture of emotions.

She was profoundly happy that Lucas would grow up in the warmth of such powerful paternal love—but at the same time it left her feeling unsettled and hollow. At one time she'd dreamed of Theo gazing at *her* with love in his eyes—now she felt confused and adrift.

Suddenly she realised that Theo was looking awkward—as if he was also finding the first time he held Lucas strange. To be fair, holding a squirming and wet six-month-old wasn't the best way to start, and she should help him. But he had taken her by surprise when he'd swooped in and plucked Lucas from out of her grasp.

She pushed herself up out of the pool, trying to keep her back to Theo and her stomach hidden as much as possible, and stepped over to the sun lounger. She held the towel up, letting it unroll so that it was covering her stretch marks, and moved closer to Theo and Lucas.

'I can take him,' she said, reaching for the baby.

'It's all right,' he said, holding on tight to Lucas. 'I've got him. Just help me get that towel round him.'

Kerry hesitated. She needed the towel to hide her stretch marks—not to mention the extra weight she was still carrying on her tummy. But she couldn't very well wrestle Lucas out of Theo's grasp.

'You can relax—I won't drop him,' Theo said caustically, obviously having misinterpreted her hesitation.

'It's not that—' Kerry started, then realised there was nothing she could say that wouldn't draw more attention to her situation.

She pressed her lips together and eased the towel around Lucas, helping Theo to get a better grip on him up against his shoulder. Then she let her hands drop and crossed her wrists self-consciously over her stomach, hoping that Theo would keep his eyes on his son.

It was a vain hope. A moment later he'd lifted his head and was looking at her over the top of Lucas's black curls. His eyes ran appreciatively down her body, just as they had done so many times before, but then suddenly they stopped, locking on to her stomach.

A slight flash of surprise lifted his black brows for

a moment. Then his eyes narrowed and his face became as dark as thunder as he continued to stare at her stretch marks.

Before she could react—turn away to hide, or pick up something to hold in front of her—she watched his expression change for the second time. From anger to disgust.

Then he spun on his heel and strode away, carrying Lucas with him.

CHAPTER EIGHT

KERRY stared after Theo, startled and hurt by what had happened. She knew her stretch marks weren't attractive, and that she hadn't completely regained her figure. But she hadn't thought she was disgusting.

Yet as she pictured Theo's face before he'd turned away, that was clearly what *he* thought about the changed appearance of her body.

Dismay welled up inside her, and she felt her cheeks grow red with shame. He'd used to look at her as if he adored her body. She knew how much pleasure he'd found in it—and had given her in return. The knowledge that he found her repulsive now that pregnancy had left its marks on her cut her to the quick.

She started following him back towards the house, feeling her heart thumping miserably.

Then, out of nowhere, a blaze of anger flared up inside her.

How *dared* he look at her like that and make her feel so horrible about herself? She'd never asked him to bring her here. She'd never asked for any of this. If life had carried on the way she'd planned she would never have laid eyes on Theo Diakos again—and *he* would never have laid his hateful, judgemental eyes on *her*.

She stormed up the grand staircase and marched through to the bedroom. The housekeeper was just carrying Lucas out of the room, chattering to him about what a lovely bathtime they would have. She watched them leaving—torn between the desire to call Sara back, so that she could bathe her son herself, and the burning need to have it out with Theo.

The door closed, leaving them completely alone for the first time since they'd come back to Greece, and she turned to face him. He was staring at her in open hostility, his eyes cutting into her like knives. Then, to add insult to injury, he deliberately let his gaze drop to her stomach and linger mercilessly on the red stretch marks.

'How *dare* you look at me like that?' she demanded, planting her hands on her hips and making no attempt to cover herself. 'How dare you try to make me feel bad over the perfectly natural way pregnancy has marked my body?'

'Just how vain and self-centred is it possible for you to be?' Theo threw up his hands in an uncharacteristically dramatic gesture, then shrugged his jacket off and tossed it angrily on the bed.

'I'm not vain!' Kerry responded hotly. 'I barely even thought about my stretch marks until you kept staring at them in disgust.'

'You think I'm disgusted with your *body*?' Theo

demanded, letting his gaze sear a trail all over her, from top to toe.

'I *know* you are,' Kerry insisted. 'I saw the expression of revulsion on your face. Well, I'm pleased—I hope you never touch me again.'

'Really?' Theo grated. He grabbed hold of her and pulled her hard up against him. 'I know that's what you want me to think—why you've been giving me the cold shoulder since we came back to Greece.'

'It's true!' Kerry gasped as he tightened his hold on her, making the breath shudder out of her body. 'I don't want you near me.'

'Let's put that to the test,' Theo taunted, suddenly sweeping her up into his arms and dumping her on the bed. 'I think you *want* me to touch you. And I don't believe you'll try to stop me, however—*wherever*—I touch you.'

'No! Let me up!' she cried, but Theo was already leaning over her, pressing her down with his hard body. His words had caused an explosion of panic inside her, but despite everything they had also started a river of molten desire running through her veins.

Lying on the bed beneath Theo, in the exact place where he had brought her to the point of rapture so many times when they were lovers, had set off a whole realm of remembered responses and feelings rocketing through her mind and body. So far he'd hardly touched her—but just the idea of him touching her was turning her on.

She stared up into his face, and the raw sexual intent she saw blazing in his dark brown eyes started her trembling deep inside. At that moment she knew that whatever common sense her mind was trying to exert, her treacherous body yearned for Theo—just as much as it always had.

'When I first saw you sitting in the pool I wanted to touch you,' Theo said. 'I wanted to slip my hands inside your bikini top and feel your nipples against my palm as I caressed your breasts.'

A hot, delicious wave of anticipation rolled through Kerry's body—but at the back of her mind warning bells were ringing. He was just playing with her—trying to humiliate her. She'd seen the way he looked at her, and heard the scornful taunts in his voice.

She reared up against him, trying to push him away and swing her legs off the bed at the same time. But Theo was ready for her, and turned her movements to his own advantage. She ended up sitting on the edge of the bed in between his legs, with her back pressed against his chest. His arm was wrapped right around her, circling her from behind, and he was leaning forward over her shoulder, with his head beside hers.

'Don't try and tell me you don't want to feel my hands on you,' he murmured, feathering the side of her neck with his hot breath.

She looked down and saw his arm around her waist, holding her securely. But his other hand was moving, brushing backwards and forwards across her midriff, getting higher and higher with each sweep. As his fingertips skimmed across her skin she felt herself shaking—awash with conflicting thoughts and emotions.

He was right—so right. She wanted to feel his hands on her. She wanted him to lie over her, possessing her, making love to her like he used to. Her pulse was racing and she was breathing erratically just from the lightest touch of his fingertips. But she didn't want it to be like this—him taunting her with her desire for him.

'You feel so good,' he breathed against her ear, sending renewed shivers quivering through her. Then his fingers slipped under the blue fabric of the bikini top and he held her breast cupped in his hand.

An involuntary sigh of delight escaped her and she arched her back, lifting her breast in subconscious invitation. His fingers moved and he gently massaged her in the way that he knew would bring her exquisite sensual pleasure.

She was hardly aware as he released his tight hold on her waist and laid her back on the bed. She didn't fight him—her eyes were closed and she was lost on a rising tide of desire. Then, when his mouth closed over her other nipple, she went rocketing into another level of arousal.

'Oh,' she breathed, momentarily forgetting everything as magical sensations spiralled out from where his tongue worked her aching nipple. 'Oh, Theo.'

Suddenly her eyes snapped open and her hands were on his shoulders, pushing him roughly away.

It was as if by saying his name out loud she had broken the spell. For a few dizzy moments she'd been in thrall to him, had lost all strength to resist—but now she was plummeting back to earth, remembering her determination to keep him at arm's length.

She stared up at him, dragging her scattered thoughts back together. Then, like a drenching with cold water, she pictured the look of disgust on his face as he stared at her stretch marks.

'You don't truly want me!' she cried, springing to her feet and staring down at him, still kneeling on the bed. 'Why are you doing this? I saw how you looked at my stretch marks.'

'You really think I care what your stretch marks look like?' Theo's voice was incredulous as he stood up next to her. 'In all the time we were together I never realised how vain and shallow you are.'

'I saw the expression on your face,' Kerry said. 'So don't try to tell me that you don't think they are horrible and ugly.'

'They're nothing!' Theo grated. 'Skin-deep, superficial lines that will soon fade. They are the marks of being a mother—you should be proud of them, not cringing and trying to hide them.'

'You don't mean that!' Kerry exclaimed. 'I saw how disgusted you looked when you saw them.'

'I was disgusted at what they represent,' Theo barked. 'Disgusted with you! With what you took from me.'

He spun away, scrubbing his hands roughly over his face as if he was in the grip of strong emotion. Then he turned back, fixing her with his piercing gaze.

'They are the marks of your pregnancy—the marks that formed because *my* son was growing inside you.'

Theo's voice was dangerously calm, but Kerry could see the fury glinting in his eyes. 'You took that from me— denied me the chance to be part of that.'

Kerry stared at him, stunned that he felt so strongly about missing out on her pregnancy. She'd never guessed it would mean so much to him.

'You should have told me,' Theo said. 'You should have told me you were pregnant.'

'I tried,' Kerry said. 'But you wouldn't listen.'

'I don't believe you,' he said. 'You never tried to contact me.'

'No, I mean...' She hesitated, suddenly realising that Theo had assumed she'd discovered her pregnancy *after* he threw her out.

Theo cursed savagely in Greek, then stormed across the room and seized her by the arms.

'You already knew!' he accused. 'You knew *before* you left Athens!'

'I tried to tell you,' she insisted. 'You wouldn't listen to me. You just told me to get out.'

'You should have made me listen,' he said. 'My God! To think you walked out of my home with my son already growing inside you!' He swore again. 'How long had you known?'

'I found out that evening,' Kerry said shakily, staring up at him nervously. It was as if a violent storm was building, towering up into a wild sky, crackling with electricity that was waiting to strike. 'I was on my way to tell you when I overheard you talking to Corban.'

Theo's eyes flared dangerously again and she realised

it had been a mistake to mention Corban, reminding Theo about the events of that awful night. Then she remembered him accusing her of dishonesty—of never being open and of deliberately keeping things from him.

There and then she vowed that he would never be able to justifiably challenge her on that score again. If this forced relationship between Theo and herself had any chance of working she could never again give him grounds to call her out on her honesty—or lack of it.

'I didn't keep on trying to tell you after the first time because I was scared,' she whispered. 'Scared of what you might do. I'd just heard you telling your brother to kidnap Nicco from his mother. I was frightened you would try to take *my* baby from *me*.'

Theo stared down at her, a muscle pulsing in his jawline and his eyes narrowed intimidatingly. The moment lengthened, and Kerry shifted her weight uneasily from one foot to the other.

'I will never try to take Lucas from you,' Theo said at last. 'In return, I expect you to be a perfect mother to him—and to the other children we will have.'

'Other children?' she gasped. 'Surely it's too early to be talking about more children?'

'Why?' he demanded. 'Do you want Lucas to be an only child? Are you not fully committed to this marriage?'

'No…it's not that.' She paused, suddenly feeling under even more pressure.

Everything had happened so quickly that she didn't know *what* to think.

'Let me assure you that *I* am fully committed to

this family,' Theo said. 'And I expect you to give me more children.'

His words rolled through her like a command, and his gaze seemed to penetrate to the centre of her being. She pressed her teeth into her lower lip and stared at him, knowing unequivocally that he was deadly serious.

'You will also be a perfect wife to me,' he added. 'In the bedroom or anywhere else I want you.' His voice was loaded with sexual intent, and his eyes skimmed meaningfully over her semi-naked body. Then he turned and walked out of the room.

Kerry swallowed reflexively and started to tremble all over again. Because she knew exactly what he meant—what he wanted from her.

A sweet dark river of anticipation began to flow along her veins, spreading out and filling every inch of her entire being with renewed desire for him. She longed to surrender her body to him again. Completely.

Later that evening, after Lucas had been put down for the night in his new nursery, Kerry strolled through the house feeling very unsettled. Theo was in his study, catching up on some work, but he'd told her he would join her for dinner. She'd showered and dressed carefully, choosing a dark blue halterneck dress and high-heeled sandals. The soft silky fabric was gathered below the bust and fell in gentle folds to just above her knees.

She wandered from room to room, thinking about everything that had happened. But it was almost impossible for her to take on board just how much her life had changed over the last few days. All she knew was that for Lucas's sake she had to find a way to make her marriage to Theo work. She knew they were compatible in the bedroom—but there was more to married life than making love and looking after children.

She was walking through the hallway when she found herself drawn to a series of paintings on the wall. Something about them seemed really familiar. Of course she knew she'd seen them lots of times before, but it was more than that.

Suddenly it came to her. They reminded her of the watercolours she had admired at Drakon's house. She tucked her hair behind her ear and looked even closer. The more she studied them, the more certain she became that they were by the same artist—and they were all of locations on Drakon's island. There was more to Theo's interest in the old man's island than he was letting on.

A few moments later she heard the door of Theo's study open. She looked up to see him coming along the corridor, rolling his shoulders as he often did when he became tense working at his computer.

A little frisson ran through her as she watched him walking towards her. He was so utterly good-looking that simply gazing at him took her breath away. He had changed out of his business suit and was dressed casually in dark jeans and a T-shirt that fitted him like a second skin. Even from that distance she could see the magnetic movement of his sculpted muscles as he walked towards her.

She realised that she had missed just looking at him

and admiring his athletic physique—marvelling in the fact that such a gorgeous man shared her bed at night.

'Ready for dinner?' he asked as he came up beside her.

'Yes,' she said, matching his mild tone. 'I'm starving. Lunch seems a long time ago.'

A little jolt shot through her as he slipped his arm around her waist, but she forced herself to relax. He clearly intended that they should put their earlier argument behind them and act like a normal couple—and she wasn't going to give him any cause for complaint.

He turned her away from the paintings and started walking towards the dining room. But at that moment she made a decision—if they were to act like a normal couple, then she ought to feel free to discuss things openly with him.

'Before we go,' she said quickly, 'I was wondering about these paintings. I'm intrigued as to why you and Drakon both have paintings by the same artist.'

Theo stopped in his tracks, and she felt him grow tense beside her.

'I'd thought that by now you would understand that I don't like people meddling or sticking their nose in where it doesn't belong,' he said. His voice was level, but she could feel displeasure emanating off him.

She turned towards him, determined that he would not over-awe her with the steely force of his personality.

'I'm not meddling,' she said, shaking her head slightly. 'I'm asking a perfectly natural question. Presumably you want Lucas to grow up with a mother who is able to have a proper conversation with his father?'

Theo looked down at her upturned face, into her wide blue eyes, surprised to realise that she was right. His response had been automatic—a knee-jerk reaction to unwanted interest in his family's difficult past. Now she was going to be part of his family, bringing up his son as a Diakos, it made sense for her to know a little about his family background—if not all of it.

In the past they had never really talked about anything personal, and now he understood that it had not turned out to be a very good basis for a relationship. If they had been more open with each other then it would not have been so easy for Kerry to keep her pregnancy from him. Trust was vital in any relationship—and he did not want her keeping secrets from him in the future.

'The paintings are the work of my uncle,' Theo said.

'Your uncle was an artist—how wonderful!' Kerry exclaimed—then she paused, her expression quizzical. 'But that means your uncle used to live on Drakon's island!' she gasped. 'Why didn't you tell me?'

'Who told you that?' Theo asked, disconcerted by how much she already seemed to know.

'No one,' Kerry said. 'I just worked it out this minute. I asked Drakon about the paintings in his house the first evening at dinner—you were late joining us because of your long walk. He told me that the artist who painted them used to live on the island.'

'That is correct,' Theo replied, unsettled to discover how close to sensitive information Kerry had strayed during her conversation with Drakon. He wondered how much the old man actually knew about the paintings and their artist.

Kerry went on. 'He said that they came with the house when he bought the island twenty-five years ago, from a property developer who'd run into financial difficulties—luckily before he'd started any building on the island.'

Theo nodded. 'That failed property developer left quite a mess when he went bankrupt—half-finished projects all over the place.'

'How fascinating,' Kerry said enthusiastically, as if her imagination was well and truly captured. 'So does that mean your uncle once owned the island?'

'Not exactly.' Theo pushed his hands through his hair and turned to walk away from the paintings, out onto the terrace that overlooked the infinity pool. 'It belonged to my mother's family. Her twin sister, my Aunt Dacia, was married to the artist.'

'What made them sell it?' Kerry asked. 'It's such a beautiful place.'

Theo frowned and looked away. He was out of his comfort zone—taken aback by how quickly Kerry was delving deeper into the story, peeling back layers that would soon reveal more than he wanted.

An ironic smile flashed across his face. His first foray into openness with his soon-to-be wife and he was already getting cold feet. It wasn't as if information about what had happened wasn't already out there in the public domain—in fact it was of very little interest to anyone but his immediate family. But it was something he preferred not to talk about—he felt shamed by association. Shamed to be his father's son.

'You don't have to tell me,' Kerry said. 'Not if you don't want to.'

She looked up at him. His black hair was spiky from where he had dragged his fingers through it and she could tell he was feeling uncomfortable. She didn't want to put him in a position he would regret later. She knew the tentative understanding they seemed to have reached could be easily broken.

She turned away, to show that she wasn't badgering him for information, and looked towards the sun going down in the western sky. They were standing overlooking the infinity pool, and in the fading light the sun-bronzed water really did seem to stretch on for ever, in a seamless sweep right out across the Aegean Sea.

This island, with its tasteful buildings and luxury swimming pools, was beautiful. But if she was completely honest it didn't have the same magic as Drakon's island. Perhaps it was the untamed wildness of that place, with its unkempt ancient olive groves and the tumbledown buildings made of natural materials. Something about that place made it truly special.

'It must have been hard for your mother and her sister to leave the island,' she said.

'My mother left by choice,' Theo replied. 'She wanted the excitement and opportunities that the mainland could offer. My aunt loved the place. She was still relatively young when her parents—my grandparents—died. But she managed to keep the place going, continuing the small business they had established making olive oil. Then she started to open her home as a retreat for painters and artists. That's how she met my uncle, Demos.'

'What made them leave?' Kerry asked. She didn't want it to seem as if she was prying, but she was genuinely interested.

'My father.' Theo's voice changed, becoming hard and unforgiving.

Kerry drew her lower lip into her mouth and looked at him apprehensively, knowing that their discussion had stumbled into hazardous territory. Now she understood why Theo had been reluctant to talk about the island—she knew he was estranged from his father, although she didn't know why.

'My father has an insatiable appetite for meddling with other people's lives,' Theo said bitterly. 'Because of his interference, my aunt and uncle lost their island. My uncle died penniless, feeling he'd failed my aunt. She was left alone, utterly broken-hearted, having lost the love of her life *and* her island home.'

'How terrible,' Kerry gasped. 'Is your aunt still alive? I've never heard you or Corban mention her.'

'That's because she won't see us,' Theo said. 'She won't have anything to do with us because of my father.'

'But it's not your fault! You aren't responsible for things your father did when you were a child,' Kerry said indignantly. 'You don't even see him any more.'

'Aunt Dacia was too badly hurt by what happened to see things rationally,' Theo said. 'For years my mother tried to help her, but she kept refusing because ultimately the money she was offering came from my father—the man she hated.'

He paused, pushing his hands through his hair once more, revealing just how unsettling he found the subject. Kerry wanted to reach out to him—to offer comfort and support. But she was scared of upsetting the fine balance they had reached.

'My father made my uncle feel inadequate because he was content to live a simple life,' Theo continued. 'He persuaded Demos and Dacia to mortgage the island and invest the money. But they weren't cut out for it. Demos was a gentle fellow, with no head for business. They lost everything.'

He turned back and looked down at her, his expression unguarded.

'My father is a dominating, powerful man,' Theo said. 'They had no chance against him. It was my mother's dying wish that her sister should have her island back.'

'And now you are trying to fulfil that wish to get back what they lost because of your father?' Kerry said quietly. 'Your aunt will be so grateful.'

'I don't know,' Theo said, with a simple shrug of his shoulders that said so much about his uncharacteristic uncertainty that Kerry felt her heart turn over in sympathy.

'Of course she will,' she said, reaching out instinctively and taking Theo's hand.

He looked down at their hands. For a moment Kerry thought that he would pull his away, that she had overstepped the mark. But then he rotated his palm against hers and threaded her fingers through his, so that they were interlocked in the way they'd always used to hold hands when they were together.

'I know how my aunt feels about my father and his money—because I feel the same way,' he said. 'All my life he interfered with my choices, tried to control me in every way. By the time I was grown up I had to get out—be my own man. I built my business up myself from scratch. I never took a single cent of his money.'

'That's amazing,' Kerry said simply. 'Lucas will be so proud that you are his father.'

Theo turned and looked down at her, feeling an unexpected ripple of emotion spread through him at her words. She had touched on a sensitive and deeply felt desire within him—that he would share the kind of relationship with his son that he had never experienced with his own father.

He wanted Lucas to grow up to love him and be proud of him. And Kerry's vote of confidence meant more to him that he would have guessed.

Her face was tilted up towards his, and she was gazing into his eyes with an open expression that took him back to a time when things had been simple between them. When they'd always seemed to be in perfect accord.

The last rays of the setting sun bathed her skin with golden light and her hair shone like satin.

'You look beautiful,' he murmured, lifting his hands to cup her face tenderly. Then he bent forward and touched his lips to hers in the lightest of kisses.

He felt a sigh of delight escape her and deepened his kiss, easing his body closer to hers and letting his hands slide into her soft silken hair. He saw her eyelids glide down and he closed his own eyes, giving himself over to the pure sensual pleasure of kissing Kerry.

Her lips were soft and yielding beneath his, and he felt her tongue lift tentatively to caress his. A rush of red-hot desire stormed through him, setting his heart thumping and the blood surging through his veins.

He needed to make love to her—right now. And this time he knew that nothing was going to stop him.

In one fluid movement he swept her up into his arms and carried her back into the house.

CHAPTER NINE

THEO strode across the hallway, carrying Kerry towards the staircase. She was as light as a feather in his arms, and felt as sexy as hell curled against his body, with one arm wrapped sensuously around his shoulder and her other hand stroking his chest.

His heart was pounding powerfully beneath her fingers and his ardour was making him feel unstoppable. He wanted to bound up the stairs to the bedroom—but at the same time he wanted the moment to last.

It felt so good to be taking Kerry to his bed, and somehow it reminded him of the first night they'd ever made love. It had been her very first time, but she'd given herself to him freely. The pure and gentle way she'd offered him her body had touched him deeply, and had made their lovemaking a thing of beauty. It felt the same way now—as if all the mistrust and anger they had been feeling towards each other was forgotten for the moment. Their desire was uncomplicated and entirely mutual.

He paused at the foot of the stairs and looked into her

wide blue eyes. Her long fringe had fallen back, away from her face, and he saw that her brow was clear and smooth. She was giving herself completely to the moment—she wanted this as much as he did.

Another surge of desire crashed through him and he bent his head to kiss her again. She reacted instantly, parting her lips to welcome his tongue into her mouth, and pulling herself up to meet him with her arms linked behind his neck.

He kissed her fiercely, revelling in the fervency of her response. She was clinging to him passionately, arching her back and thrusting her breasts against his chest. He heard her moan and felt her trembling—and he knew it was time to get to the privacy of the bedroom. Or he wouldn't be able to stop himself from making love to her right there in the hall.

He took the stairs two at a time and strode into the bedroom, kicking the door shut with his foot. For a moment his eyes settled on the king-sized bed across the room. Ever since Kerry had left the bedroom had seemed empty and cold. But now he had brought her back, to make this room into a place of vibrancy and life. A place of hot, hard passion.

He felt her flex impatiently in his arms, asking with her body to be put down. Then she was standing face to face with him—only inches away, but far enough so that he could look down into her lovely face.

He could see that her colour was high, her breathing was rapid and her blue eyes were almost black with the power of her desire for him. His own body was throbbing with his need, and he pulled her roughly towards him once more, plundering her mouth with his and letting his hands run wild over her supple body. What had started with a gentle kiss in the glow of the sunset had rapidly accelerated into a vortex of unbridled passion. He couldn't stop now even if he wanted to.

Kerry gasped for breath and pulled back from Theo's kiss, staring up into his flushed face through a haze of feverish excitement. Her entire body was trembling, yearning for him to make love to her. She could tell how much he wanted her, and that knowledge had unleashed an answering torrent of desire within her.

When he'd swept her up the stairs and into the bedroom she'd felt like a new bride being carried over the threshold. At the back of her mind she knew that things weren't like that. But she pushed those thoughts aside and gave in to the sheer happiness of being back in Theo's arms.

It was so long since they'd made love that she almost felt like a virgin again. All her memories of how wonderful it had been seemed too good to be true, as if they were simply wild fantasies. But now she was going to experience Theo's physical love once more.

'You look so good,' Theo said, letting his eyes roam over her as she stood in front of him, wearing a backless dress that skimmed over her curves.

His words sent a wave of confidence running through her, and she reached up to unfasten the halterneck. The fine midnight-blue fabric slipped through her fingers, and a moment later the garment was pooled in a circle around her feet.

'Now you look even better.'

From the way his deep voice caught in his throat, Kerry knew that he liked what he saw. Feeling even bolder, she walked towards him in her high-heeled sandals, just wearing a lacy bra and matching French knickers.

'You are wearing too many clothes,' she said huskily, pulling his T-shirt up and over his head. As his bronzed torso came into view she sucked in a shuddering breath of pure appreciation. He was mouth-wateringly well formed, with perfect satiny skin that made her want to lean forward and run her tongue across his muscled chest, to put her face as close as possible to his beating heart.

She stared at him, feeling her breathing growing faster again. Rampant desire was rushing through her, and suddenly she needed to feel his hands on her again.

As if he had read her mind, he reached out to her and pulled her into his arms. Then his hands were skimming down her back, curving over her bottom, running back up between her shoulderblades to her bra clasp.

With one expert flick he undid the flimsy garment, then cast it aside and pulled her to him. Skin on skin. Hot, hard muscle pressed to tingling, sensitive breasts. With every heaving breath she took her nipples moved against him. The delicious friction of his chest hair rubbing across their throbbing points was driving her to distraction.

She curved sinuously against him, needing to feel more of him. His hands were moving downwards again, and this time he hooked his thumbs into her French knickers. He tugged them past her hips, and then her last remaining item of clothing fell to the floor.

With a deep breath of pent-up excitement she stepped out of her knickers and slipped off her sandals at the same time. She was completely naked.

Theo's dark eyes swept over her, leaving a trail of tingling anticipation prickling over her skin. But she wanted more—she needed more.

'Touch me,' she pleaded. 'Put your hands on me.'

He needed no further encouragement, and in an instant he was standing behind her, skimming his hands around the sensitive skin of her midriff. His chest was pressed against her back, warm and solid behind her, but all she could think about was the wonderful way he was touching her.

As she felt his hands sliding upwards over her ribs, she instinctively looked down at herself. The sight of her own naked breasts, jiggling slightly with the trembling of her body and the rapid rate of her breathing, startled her. Her nipples were jutting forward, taut and throbbing with the need for his attention, and even looking at them herself seemed to make them ache even more.

Suddenly his hands curved up and over her breasts, and a shuddering sigh escaped her. He massaged her tender flesh, sending waves of sensual pleasure rolling through her. Then he teased her nipples gently between his fingers and thumbs, and the pleasure intensified.

Her head fell back against his shoulder and she closed her eyes. It felt so perfect standing there, feeling the skin of her back pressed against his solid chest while his hands created marvellous sensations, spiralling out from her breasts.

Then he lifted one hand to sweep her hair to the side, baring her neck so that he could lean forward and kiss the sensitive skin below her ear. He nuzzled her and she wriggled against him, as a ticklish shower of sexually charged sensations feathered through her, sending her pulse-rate soaring.

She was breathing rapidly, and every gasping breath renewed her awareness of his hand on her breast—of the glorious pleasure he was creating with his touch. But his other hand was moving again, sliding downwards, towards the most sensitive part of her body.

She parted her legs slightly, instinctively rocking her pelvis forward as his hand slipped between her thighs, seeking the throbbing core of her arousal.

'Oh, Theo!' His name burst out of her as his fingers made contact, and as his fingertips caressed her pulsing centre the pleasure was almost too great. She bucked against him, aware only of the blood singing in her ears and the impossibly intense sensations shooting out from where he stroked her.

Her legs turned to jelly and she started to sink downwards, but he swept her up into his arms just in time and carried her to the bed.

Suddenly she couldn't wait any longer to feel him lying over her, thrusting into her, taking her out of her body and into the heavens beyond. She reached feverishly for his belt, and with shaky, uncoordinated movements pulled the supple black leather through the loops on his jeans, then unfastened the buckle.

She moaned—a low, almost feral sound—and struggled desperately with the button, then the zipper. She could feel his erection thrusting powerfully against the fabric of his jeans and she wanted, *needed* him to be totally naked—but her hands were trembling too much for her to manage.

Theo pushed her hands aside with movements that betrayed a sense of urgency that matched Kerry's. Then he rolled from the bed to kick his jeans off himself.

For a moment he stood looking down at her. The sexual hunger that shone from his dark eyes made her quiver with anticipation. She couldn't lie still—the overwhelming need she felt for him was too great.

She pushed herself up on her elbows, aware of every part of her body, from her tingling nipples to her trembling legs, and looked up into his handsome face, knowing that her desire for him must be written all over her features.

Then he came towards her, moving across her body with power and grace. She reached up and looped her arms around him, delighting in the broad, masculine strength of his back. Her thighs fell apart and her hips tilted upwards, ready to welcome his intimate possession of her willing body.

'Oh!' She cried out as he pressed forward and she felt his hard length sliding smoothly inside her. A wave of pleasure washed over her and she lifted her legs, wrapping them tightly round his hips, pulling him deeper still. He paused for a moment, driving her almost wild with unfulfilled need, and then he started to move.

She clung to him, flying higher and higher. Every masterful thrust of his hips brought a surge of wonderful sensation powering through her that quickly blocked out everything but the present.

All those long lonely nights when she'd wondered if Theo's lovemaking could possibly be as amazing as she remembered were forgotten. The only thing that existed for her now was the all-consuming pleasure of being one with him.

She could hear his breathing getting harder, and her own breath was coming in shallow, moaning gasps.

The pleasure within her was tightening, growing more and more focussed. Suddenly her shoulders lifted off the bed, her back arched and her inner muscles clenched tight around his hardness. She had reached the pinnacle of delight and she gasped for breath, her world exploding into a rapturous kaleidoscope of colours.

A second later, from deep within the glow of her climax, she heard Theo shout as he stormed towards his zenith. He reared up above her and gave a mighty shudder as he reached his moment of release.

A shaft of silvery moonlight shone across the room as Kerry lay quietly on the bed, listening to the sound of Theo breathing. Even in sleep his presence seemed to fill the room. But now, for the first time since he'd come back into her life, Kerry was basking in it. She just wanted to lie there and soak up the warmth radiating off the magnificent man next to her.

The embers of her orgasm were still glimmering inside her, diffusing an amazing sense of fulfilment throughout her body. And, even more wonderfully, she felt hopeful for her future with Theo.

She knew that the conversation they'd had right before Theo had swept her upstairs had helped to change the atmosphere between them. He'd been so candid and it had touched her deeply. It was a change in him that she hoped would continue. Not that they'd been dishonest in their communication before—but they'd both held back too much.

She knew that she'd been reserved and guarded—too worried by what Theo would think if she was completely open with him.

But she'd been hurt so many times throughout her childhood, culminating in the most horrible shock when she was eighteen. So she'd taught herself not to expect too much from other people. Not to ask for anything because it would inevitably lead to disappointment.

She had continued to live by that philosophy when she first met Theo—being grateful for their time together but never asking for more. And never burdening him with anything that was troubling her.

But that was going to change. Now she was going to follow Theo's lead and take down her protective barriers. He had done it, and it had made them closer. But she knew they could be closer still.

Very early the following morning Kerry brought Lucas downstairs to give him a drink of milk. He'd always woken up at the crack of dawn, and nothing seemed to be changing about that since they'd arrived in Greece.

As she walked outside onto the terrace she saw that Theo was swimming. She sat at the table with Lucas on her lap as Theo powered through the water beside them. She never tired of watching him—he was a natural swimmer, and he seemed to glide at super-speed through the water with the effortless strength of a dolphin.

It was a beautiful morning—still so early that the sea was a shimmering silver-blue and the sky was tinged pale apricot from the recent sunrise. Kerry felt good—genuinely happy that Theo had brought her back here with him.

He finished his lengths and lifted his head, noticing her for the first time. She lifted her hand to wave at him as he swam over to the steps—just as she had done so many times in the past.

A strange feeling washed over her. Maybe it was still the afterglow of their lovemaking—or the positive effect of their conversation the evening before. But she felt as if she was home. As if she belonged here.

Theo reached the steps and surged out of the pool, water pouring off the hard planes of his muscled body. He looked like a Greek god emerging from the sea, and Kerry felt a renewed kick of desire deep inside.

'Good morning.' Her voice sounded huskier than normal, and she smiled up at him, suddenly feeling shy.

'Hello,' he said, towelling himself off roughly and coming to stand beside the table. 'How are you this morning? And Lucas?'

'We're very well, thank you,' she said.

She drew in a shaky breath as she looked up at his magnificent masculine body, wondering what he was planning for the day—whether or not he had to fly to Athens again. She felt so different from yesterday, when she'd been glad that he'd had to leave the island.

'I'm going to shower,' he said. 'And then I'd like to spend some time with you and Lucas—if that suits you.'

'That would be lovely,' Kerry said, feeling a warm glow of expectation spreading through her.

Theo emerged from the shower feeling fully energised, thinking about making love with Kerry the night before. It had been good. Incredible, actually. If their marriage was going to work, that was the way they should always make love. Openly and honestly. Untainted by their troubles outside the bedroom.

When they'd arrived on the island Kerry had been so withdrawn—moody, even, although she'd barely spoken—he'd started to have serious concerns for their future. But now she seemed to have snapped out of it, and their situation seemed to be more manageable.

The sound of his phone ringing cut into his thoughts.

'Diakos,' he barked, annoyed with his PA for calling him so early. It had better be important...

Two minutes later he stormed through the house in a black temper. He strode out of the terrace doors and nearly collided with Kerry coming the other way, not looking where she was going because she was chattering away to the baby.

'Oh!' Kerry gasped, clutching Lucas tightly as she wobbled, grateful for Theo's steadying hold on her arm.

'All right?' Theo asked, slowly releasing his grip.

'Yes. Thank you,' Kerry replied, looking up into his face. His dark expression made her catch her breath. 'Are *you* all right? You look like you've had bad news.'

'I'm fine,' Theo replied shortly. 'But I *have* had some bad news.'

He looked at her sharply for a moment, then led her into the living room and sat with her on the sofa.

'It's Drakon,' he said. 'I'm afraid he's taken a turn for the worse. He's in hospital in Athens.'

'Oh, no—poor Drakon!' Kerry gasped. 'How serious is it?'

'I'm not sure,' Theo replied. 'My PA is trying to find out more information. I'll let you know when I hear anything.'

'We must send something,' Kerry said, feeling tears prick her eyes. Drakon loved his island home so much that the thought of him lying in a city hospital was awful. 'Can we visit him?'

'I'll try to find out,' Theo said.

Later that day they heard the good news that Drakon's condition was improved. In fact he had asked for Theo to visit him in hospital, to discuss the sale of the island.

'He must be feeling better,' Kerry said, a smile of relief spreading across her pale face.

'Yes,' Theo agreed, although he wasn't so hopeful as Kerry.

He leafed through the documents he had just thrust into his briefcase, trying to keep his expression bland. Kerry seemed to have become so attached to the old man that he didn't want to risk her getting in a state. He had to leave for Athens as soon as possible.

He wasn't as naive as Kerry. He had the feeling that Drakon was putting his affairs in order. That he wanted the sale to go through quickly so that his daughter was not left vulnerable to property sharks after his death.

'You should tell Drakon why you want the island,' Kerry said suddenly. 'Then he would definitely sell to you.'

'He *is* going to sell to me,' Theo replied flatly, feeling a nasty jab of irritation at Kerry's unexpected comment. 'Mine is the best offer he's received.'

'But it's not about the money,' Kerry insisted. 'You told me that. He cares about the island.'

'Don't give me business advice.' Theo's voice was bitingly cold. 'Don't think that because I took you to his island you are in any way qualified to offer me your opinion.'

He stared at her angrily. Why had she become so bold all of a sudden? The girl who'd shared his life before would never have started trying to tell him how to manage his business affairs.

'I'm thinking about Drakon,' Kerry said crossly.

She met his hostile stare square-on, unable to believe how cold he was being. Her eyes flashed over him, standing tall and stiff in his dark business suit, and once again she felt as distant from him as she'd ever been.

She'd never got involved in his work before, even when she'd been present at business dinners or overheard him discussing work matters. She'd always known that it was not her concern and that Theo would not welcome her input.

But that timid young girl had changed. Maybe it was the fact that she was a mother now, and had spent the last six months fending for herself and her baby, making decisions that impacted on another little person's life as well as her own.

Or maybe it was because a year ago Theo had heartlessly severed their relationship and thrown her out onto the streets, making her realise how little respect he had for her.

Whatever the reason, she found she couldn't stand by silently any more.

'An old man is lying sick in a hospital bed,' she said passionately. 'And you have the power to make him feel good about the one thing that really matters to him—his island.'

'It's none of his business *why* I want the island,' Theo replied.

'He has devoted the last twenty-five years of his life to preserving that island,' Kerry snapped. 'If he knew that you wanted it for your aunt—so she could live simply, in harmony with the place—think how much that would mean to him.'

'That's not the way I do business,' Theo snapped. 'With rose-coloured idealistic drivel. I deal with hard financial business plans.'

'Don't be so hypocritical,' she said hotly. 'This isn't *normal* business for you. You're not looking for a profit. You told me yourself that you want the island to fulfil your mother's dying wish—so that your aunt can have her home back.'

'I'm not about to share my family's past shame with a stranger,' Theo snapped. 'We don't air our dirty linen in public.'

'You don't have to tell him everything,' Kerry said in exasperation. 'Just say your aunt wishes to live there quietly.'

'I didn't have to tell *you* everything—and I'm already regretting that I did,' Theo said bitterly, slamming his briefcase shut and striding angrily towards the door. 'By now, after everything that has happened, *you* of all people should understand that in this family we keep our personal problems private. We keep things in the family.'

Kerry stared at him as he stood in the doorway, glaring back at her. Suddenly the unmistakable sound of a helicopter approaching the island caught her attention—and her memory flashed back to the conversation she'd overheard on the night Theo had thrown her out.

He had told Corban to take Nicco away to the island by helicopter, without his mother's knowledge. Then he'd said they'd deal with Hallie privately—no one outside the family needed to know.

'Like Hallie,' Kerry cried. 'Hallie was a problem. So you planned to take her son and deal with her in private.'

'It would have been better for everyone if that had

happened,' Theo bit out. He raked his hand roughly through his hair and came back into the room, shutting the door behind him.

Kerry felt a wave of anxiety roll through her as she looked up at his livid expression. What had made him close the door, even though the helicopter was waiting for him outside?

'Hallie is an alcoholic,' Theo said. 'And Corban was desperate to take care of her. But instead of accepting the best care in a private facility abroad she crashed her car, with Nicco in it, on the busiest square in Athens, narrowly missing a souvenir stall surrounded by tourists. There was quite an audience when the ambulance men pulled her from the car, crying that her husband planned to steal her child from her.'

'Is that what stopped you taking Nicco?' Kerry gasped.

'No,' Theo grated. 'It stopped Corban putting her quietly in rehab, which was where she needed to be—for her own sake and for Nicco's sake. With all the media attention her recovery was much slower than it should have been. Your interference nearly broke up their marriage—not to mention causing what might have been a tragic accident.'

Kerry stared up at him, suddenly speechless. Was he telling the truth? That Hallie was an alcoholic? That he and Corban had simply been planning the best way to help her? Had she jumped to the wrong conclusions—putting everyone at risk and causing a whole barrage of problems for the family?

'Because you are the mother of my son, you will soon

be part of this family,' Theo said. 'But if you want to stay—be part of Lucas's life—never interfere again.'

'Don't threaten me,' Kerry said shakily. 'You can't take Lucas from me.'

'Yes, I can.' Theo said coldly. 'And if you cross me I will. Never doubt that for a second.'

He turned and strode out of the door, leaving Kerry staring after him in shock.

CHAPTER TEN

THE heavy aroma of flowering jasmine hung in the air as Kerry pushed Lucas's buggy through the streets near Kolonaki Square, passing designer stores and chic cafés filled with elegant Athenian ladies and well-heeled businessmen.

The floral fragrance was typical of Athens, and it reminded Kerry painfully of her first summer in the city—when Theo had swept her off her feet and she'd fallen head over heels in love with him.

She'd never stood a chance. His charm, his amazing good-looks and the irresistible force of his personality had totally overwhelmed her. At the time she'd believed she was blissfully happy with him—but she'd been living in a dream world. Now she knew their relationship had been harmonious simply because she'd gone along with everything he wanted, never doing anything to upset the balance. Never asking for anything.

As she looked back on that summer, Kerry realised a more confident, experienced woman might not have been so in awe of him—might have realised that the relationship was completely superficial. But Kerry had been too in love to see beyond the joy she'd felt just being with Theo.

She knew that some people wanted to spend their lives enjoying the present, with no thought for the future—but she wasn't one of them. As a child she'd longed to be part of a warm, loving family, and that was what she so desperately wished to give Lucas. But now it seemed to be an impossible hope—every day Theo seemed to become even more distant from her.

They'd returned to Athens, and preparations were underway for a quiet family wedding, but communication between them was limited to brief, impersonal exchanges about Lucas. She longed to talk to him properly, to try and improve the atmosphere between them. But their last argument had been so terrible that she was afraid to disturb the uneasy equilibrium they'd reached.

At least she now understood why Theo had been so blindingly furious with her the night Hallie had crashed her car—but the reason made her feel dejected and guilt-ridden. It wasn't just that she'd interfered—questioning Theo's intentions and challenging his command—it was because he truly believed that he'd been doing the right thing for the people he loved. He couldn't even begin to understand why she had gone against him.

But Kerry had never guessed Hallie was an alcoholic. Looking back on it, she realised the signs had been there. But as she'd usually only seen her friend on social occasions it had never occurred to her that Hallie drank a lot—and she knew that sometimes alcoholics became very good at concealing their problem. It was also likely that Theo and Corban had done their best to hide it, thinking that by keeping it in the family they were doing the right thing—but if Kerry had known she would never have made such a terrible mistake.

She returned to the hotel with a heavy heart. She felt so sorry for what had happened—*for what she had done*—but she didn't know how to talk to Theo about it. However, she did know that the problem was not going to go away on its own. It was always going to be there, creating a chasm between them.

She took the elevator up to the family's luxury apartments and got Lucas ready for his nap.

'Time for a sleep, my little angel,' she said, laying him carefully in his cot.

He settled almost immediately, and she wandered out onto the balcony, drawn by the sounds of splashing and laughing floating up to her. She looked down to the private terrace of Corban's apartment and saw Corban, Hallie and Nicco, all playing in the pool. They were back from their trip.

A wave of emotion rolled through her. They all looked so joyful. Nicco had grown so much, Hallie was pregnant again and the love and pride Corban felt for his family shone out of his face.

They were all together, having fun, enjoying each other's company. It was the perfect family moment. And because of her that moment might never have been able to happen.

Suddenly her throat felt tight and her eyes filled with moisture. The next second she burst into tears.

Theo strode through the hotel on his way up to see Kerry. His staff had informed him—as they always did—that she'd returned to the hotel, and he wanted to tell her that Corban and Hallie had arrived home from their travels.

He did not want her to stumble across them inadvertently, possibly creating an awkward situation. It was his intention to be present the first time they encountered each other, so that a potentially tricky moment would be under his control.

He walked through their apartment quietly, in case Lucas was asleep, and found Kerry standing on the balcony looking down at the terrace below. Something about her body language pricked his attention immediately. Her shoulders were drawn in and she was shaking.

Suddenly he realised she was weeping.

'Kerry?' He spoke her name quietly, but she spun round at once, her face an open book of remorse.

'I'm sorry,' she sobbed. 'Oh, Theo—I'm so sorry for what I did that night.'

The pure emotion in her voice cut into him disconcertingly—but he told himself it didn't matter what she said, how she tried to defend her actions. He knew he would never forgive her for what she'd done. She'd deliberately betrayed his plans—putting both his sister-in-law and his nephew in danger.

'I did something inexcusable—something terrible.'

Her voice rose urgently. 'But I never meant harm to come to anyone. You have to know that wasn't my intention.'

'I have no idea what you intended,' Theo said honestly. He'd racked his brain repeatedly—wondering what had possessed her to go running to Hallie. Surely she'd known him well enough to realise that he only ever wanted what was best for his family. 'What in God's name were you thinking?'

He stared at her, feeling all the anger he'd tried to put aside for Lucas's sake rising up within him once more.

'I was thinking about my mother,' Kerry suddenly blurted. 'I was thinking about how it killed her!' She dragged in a tortured breath and turned away from him, covering her face with her hands.

Theo stared at her in shock. What was she talking about? What did the death of Kerry's mother have to do with what had happened the night Hallie crashed the car?

'They took my mother's baby away.' Kerry's words were muffled, but Theo could just about hear what she was saying. 'They took *me* away from my mother—and it destroyed her.'

She scrubbed her palms over her face, then turned round to look at him again. He could see just how badly talking about—even *thinking* about—her mother was affecting Kerry. Her face was pale and her eyes wide, and her whole body was shaking violently.

'Come inside and sit down,' he said, reaching out towards her.

She curled in on herself and shrank away from him—

as if at that moment she couldn't bear to be touched. But then she edged past him and walked unevenly to the sofa.

For a moment Theo hesitated, then he poured her a glass of cold water and sat down next to her.

Kerry picked up the water automatically with a trembling hand and took a sip. It was the first time she had ever spoken about her mother to anyone. Her heart was thumping and her palms felt damp and clammy.

She didn't want to say anything else—what would Theo think when he knew the truth about her?—but now she had started she knew she had to finish.

'My mother was very young when she had me,' Kerry said. 'Only sixteen.'

She paused, glancing at him to see if he seemed shocked—but his expression was unreadable.

'My grandmother was horrified. She forced my mother to hand me over to her, so she could bring me up alongside Bridget, her other, much younger daughter,' Kerry said. 'But it was a disaster for everyone. She never really wanted me, and always resented having an extra child to take care of. But even worse, her decision to take me destroyed my mother's life. It made her feel like a failure and she never managed to get her life on track.'

She paused again, and took another sip of water to steady her nerves. Now she was telling Theo she felt really strange—almost as if she was watching someone else telling their life story.

'So Bridget is really your aunt,' Theo said. 'But you were brought up together, by the same person.'

'I *think* of her as my sister,' she replied. 'We grew up with each other and there's not much age difference between us.' She rubbed her hands over her face and took a few steadying breaths. Now she had started, she had to tell the final, most awful piece of the story.

'Maybe if my mother had had her child to look after, she would've had a purpose in life—a reason to sort herself out,' Kerry continued. 'As it was, she turned to drink and then started taking drugs. She died of an overdose in the end.'

'I'm sorry,' Theo said. 'That must have been very hard for you.'

'At the time I thought she was my much older sister,' Kerry said. 'I didn't even know her because Mum—I mean my grandmother—threw her out after I was born and wouldn't let her back in the house. I met her once or twice when I was little, but I barely remember it.'

For the first time Kerry detected a response in Theo—and she lifted her eyes to see a look of shock on his face.

'She didn't tell you who your mother was? She lied to you?' he asked incredulously.

'My grandmother said it was in everyone's best interests,' Kerry said bitterly. 'Really she was covering up the shame she felt because her teenage daughter had had a baby. I only found out when I was eighteen years old. I needed my birth certificate to apply for a passport when I got a job in the travel agency.'

She shuddered, hugging herself as she remembered

the utter shock she'd felt as she'd looked at the birth certificate, staring in disbelief and confusion at her older sister's name, written clearly in the section for her mother's name.

By then she'd already been dead. It hadn't been possible for Kerry to get to know her. Her grandmother, an embittered, mean-spirited woman, who hadn't even wanted to look after her in the first place, had denied her the right to get to know her mother.

It was only when her eyes blurred with tears that Kerry realised she was weeping again. Theo was beside her in an instant, this time pulling her into his arms and holding her to his broad chest.

She leant into his embrace, taking comfort from the strong, regular heartbeat below her cheek. It meant so much that he hadn't pulled away from her in disgust when he'd heard her story. She knew it was a lot for anyone to take in—and now he had discovered that the mother of his son came from a truly messed-up family.

'I'm sorry,' she said. 'I'm sorry that I haven't given Lucas a better background.'

'Don't apologise for things that are not your fault. I would never blame you or think less of you because of your background,' Theo said, stroking her hair gently away from her tear-streaked face. 'Things like that mean nothing to me. I only care that our son has what he needs—love from both his parents.' He paused, cupping her chin softly and tipping her head back so he could look down into her eyes. 'Lucas will never be short of love.'

A wave of warmth washed through her at his words. She knew he was speaking sincerely—and she knew that he really did not judge her for her troubled background.

It felt as if an enormous weight had been lifted off her shoulders, and for the first time she felt that Theo was looking at her and seeing the whole truth about the person she really was. Until that moment she had never realised what a heavy burden the secret of her background had been.

'I'm glad you told me,' Theo said, sliding his fingers through her hair to the nape of her neck.

He looked down at her, finally understanding what had driven her to react so recklessly to the conversation she had overheard the night of the accident. He meant what he had said—he would never judge anyone according to their background. After all, he would hate to be judged on the basis of being his father's son.

But it was terrible to think about Kerry growing up in such difficult circumstances. It was no wonder she'd never talked about her past.

'I can't face seeing Hallie and Corban again,' Kerry said. Then she bit her lip, realising how cowardly that sounded. She couldn't hide from her mistake for ever. She had to face up to it and take responsibility for what she had done.

'I'll be with you,' Theo said, drawing her towards him with his hand behind her head.

'Thank you.' Kerry looked up at him, wondering if

that meant he thought there would be trouble. Theo had been angry with her—surely Corban would be too? It was his wife and child that Kerry had endangered.

'Don't think about it now,' Theo said, bending his head and pressing his mouth to her cheek with the lightest of touches. 'Don't think about anything.'

A ripple of pleasure ran through her and she closed her eyes, feeling him kissing her again and again. The touch of his lips was as light as a shower of raindrops, scattering over her face to wash away her tears.

It felt wonderful—just knowing there were no more secrets between them. For the first time ever she could truly let down her guard. Theo knew all about her—and yet he was still here with her, kissing her, caressing her…starting to make love to her.

She sighed with delight and leant into his embrace, opening her lips as he finally kissed her on the mouth. Her pulse rate leapt up as his tongue slid inside, setting off a cascade of feelings surging through her body.

Suddenly she was burning with desire for him. She was hot and desperate to feel his body moving against hers, to feel his hands on her bare skin.

She grappled with his clothing urgently, pulling and tugging—and he was undressing her at the same time. Then all at once they were both standing naked, devouring each other with their eyes.

'You look so good,' she murmured, startled by how husky her voice sounded. For a second she didn't move, just stood there letting her eyes roam freely over his magnificent body. He was fully aroused and ready for her, and his erection drew her gaze like a magnet. Her breathing was becoming ragged just from looking at him—but she wanted the moment to last.

His eyes were on her too, searing a tingling trail over the peaks of her breasts, down across her stomach to the soft curls at the apex of her legs—and the expression of erotic hunger on his face was turning her on even more.

Then suddenly he stepped towards her, as if he was unable to keep his hands off her a moment longer, and her world exploded into a wild, sexual tangle of entwined limbs and kissing mouths.

Hot, liquid arousal sang through her veins and rang in her ears, blotting out everything but her growing need to feel Theo lying over her, thrusting long and hard into her body. But suddenly she found herself leaning back on the sofa, with him kneeling between her legs.

She barely had time to anticipate the exquisite rapture he was about to deliver, when his mouth came down on her. She let out a shuddering cry as his tongue and lips caressed her most sensitive, intimate place, setting wave after wave of pure sexual sensation rolling through her. Her whole body was suffused with pulsing pleasure and she felt herself rocketing upwards, straight towards a shattering, all-encompassing climax.

She cried out as she reached a moment of release, but before she had a chance to drift back down Theo had lifted himself over her and thrust his hard, masculine length deep into her body.

Her trembling, sensitised flesh clamped around him,

and she shot back up into the heavens immediately. She hadn't known it was possible to feel such intense sensual pleasure—but Theo drove her higher and higher. Thrusting deeper and deeper into her willing body, he carried her up and up until she was lost in a whirling vortex of pure sexual excitement.

Then, as the final crescendo of delirious ecstasy crashed through her, she heard Theo shout as he reached his own explosive climax.

Kerry smiled tenderly as she looked at Theo lying beside her. Her body was still glowing from their lovemaking, and her heart felt a gladness she could never remember feeling before. She had told Theo about her past—about all the sordid details of her dysfunctional family—and he still wanted to be with her.

She knew it was for Lucas's sake, but she finally felt as if she and Theo were growing closer. She didn't think that he had fully forgiven her for what she had done, but at least now he understood *why* she had not been thinking clearly the night of the accident.

She lifted her hand and traced her fingers gently over the contours of his gorgeous face—across his high cheekbones and down to his strong, angular jaw. He opened his dark brown eyes and looked at her, his sensual lips curving into a lazy smile as his gaze held hers, filling her with another wave of warmth.

'You look beautiful,' he said, his voice low and husky.

She smiled, feeling the flutter of butterflies deep inside her. Just looking at him made her feel good—joyful and excited at the same time. Her blood tingled through her veins like champagne. She was so happy to be there with him—so happy that he was the father of her child.

Suddenly her heart turned over and she realised something—something wonderful and terrible at the same time.

She loved him. She had fallen in love with Theo all over again.

Later that day Theo took Kerry to meet Hallie and Corban. Her legs felt weak with nerves, but she knew she had to overcome them. Not just for the sake of her future in the Diakos family—but because it was the right thing to do.

'I'm so sorry for what I did.' Kerry rushed the words out the moment they were all together.

They seemed to jar uncomfortably around the room, as if she'd just said something out of place, and she felt her stomach crunch with nervous agitation. But in her heart she knew there was no point waiting, working awkwardly through small talk, with such a big issue still hanging in the air between them.

'It's all right,' Hallie said suddenly, throwing her arms around Kerry impulsively. 'Everyone is all right.'

'But…but when I think what might have happened…' Kerry stammered, feeling her eyes brimming with tears of remorse. She'd thought that after her afternoon of confession with Theo she was all cried out—but as the tears ran down her cheeks she knew that she wasn't.

'Honestly, I can't remember much about it,' Hallie

said. 'But I know you—I know you didn't mean to harm anyone. Maybe you even helped me, in a way.'

'I don't understand,' Kerry said, gratefully taking the tissue Hallie offered her and dabbing her eyes.

'I don't think I was ready to accept that I needed help,' Hallie said. 'I know it wasn't the best way to realise that I did—but at least crashing the car made me stop and think.'

'But...but...' Kerry wasn't ready to believe that anything good could have come of that night.

'You didn't put the car keys in my hand,' Hallie said. 'But you did try to stop me—and you went straight for help.'

She turned and reached out her arm for her husband, drew him closer to them.

'We forgive you,' Hallie said. 'And we are pleased that you will be part of the family again.'

Kerry smiled tremulously as she looked at Hallie. She was such a kind, generous soul, and Kerry felt so grateful. Hallie's friendship had always meant a lot to her, and she knew that it would enrich her life now that she was to be married to Theo.

'Theo has told me what happened.' Corban's deep voice rumbled beside her and she turned to look up at him. He was so like his brother that when his dark eyes met hers she felt a rush of nervousness. 'I accept that you did not mean for any harm to come to my family.'

Despite his words of assurance there was no warmth in his eyes. Kerry knew that he was still protective towards his wife and child—and she understood why.

The fact that Hallie had forgiven her so freely was more than enough. She knew she would have to earn Corban's trust again, but for his brother's sake he was prepared to accept her into the family.

'Thank you.' Kerry spoke sincerely.

'Let's go for dinner.' Hallie's voice was bright and breezy, and Kerry knew she was determined to lighten the atmosphere, to put the past behind them. 'You can tell me all about the wedding plans.'

Theo fell into step with his brother as they walked through into the dining room, but his eyes were on Kerry. She was clearly relieved that seeing Hallie and Corban again had gone so well—and Theo shared that relief.

He wasn't in the habit of worrying about what other people thought, but he realised he'd been ill at ease, waiting for this meeting to take place.

Perhaps it was because up until this afternoon Kerry had never truly apologised for what had happened. He'd only known that she regretted the outcome—rather than the fact that she had interfered in the first place. But now he believed that she was genuinely sorry. And he'd been impressed by the open honesty she had shown Hallie and Corban.

As he looked at her a strange sensation passed through him. He frowned, momentarily disconcerted as he couldn't identify what he was feeling. Then he realised what it was—pride. He was proud of how she had taken responsibility and given such a heartfelt apology to Hallie and Corban.

CHAPTER ELEVEN

OVER the next few weeks Kerry re-established her friendship with Hallie. They'd always got along well, and it was wonderful to have someone to pass the time with while Theo was working. It was good for the children to play together too. Lucas, who had just started crawling, had great fun following his older cousin Nicco around.

The wedding came and went with the minimum of fuss. It was a small ceremony, just for immediate family, and afterwards Theo took Kerry and Lucas to the island for a couple of days. She was a little disappointed that he'd only taken such a small amount of time out of his busy schedule for them. Not that she'd wanted a big fancy honeymoon, but she would have liked the chance to spend more time with Theo. She finally felt as if they were starting to get to know each other again, but it was slow progress because he was always working.

When they returned to Athens, Corban and Hallie had already left to continue the trip they had interrupted to attend the wedding. Kerry and Lucas were alone during the day once again, and life settled into a quiet pattern.

One day, about a week later, Kerry received a message from Drakon, asking her to come and see him at the hospital. She was surprised because Theo had told her that he wasn't well enough for visitors—and hadn't been for some time. In fact the afternoon that Theo had flown from the island to meet Drakon at the hospital the old man had taken another turn for the worse. Theo had been refused access and the situation with the sale of the island was still unresolved.

Kerry looked at the handwritten note that Drakon had sent to her. She had the feeling that Theo would not be pleased if she went to see the old man alone—but he'd flown to Paris that morning and wouldn't be back till late. She didn't want to keep Drakon waiting. His health seemed so precarious that he might not be fit to see her if she delayed her visit.

So she left Lucas with the housekeeper and went to the hospital alone.

'Thank you for coming,' Drakon said, struggling to sit up straighter against the starched white hospital pillows. 'I wasn't sure if you'd be able to.'

'Of course I came,' Kerry said, crossing the room to kiss Drakon lightly on the cheek. She was startled by how changed he seemed—he looked so frail that she'd hardly recognised him at first.

'There are a few things I want to ask you,' he said, getting straight down to business. 'Forgive me for not worrying about the social niceties—but I tire easily.'

Kerry looked at the old man, suddenly feeling wary. She had a feeling that she wasn't going to want to answer his questions…

Theo signed the last of the documents securing his purchase of Drakon's island and stepped back, away from the old man's hospital bed.

'You take care of my island,' Drakon instructed him testily. 'And take care of that pretty wife of yours. You've got a gem there—although I think you're too pig-headed to realise it.'

Theo looked down at the old man, biting back the cutting retort that had come into his mind. The island was his now—he did not have to answer to anybody about what he chose to do with it. And—unfortunately—he was well aware of what kind of woman he had married.

'Trust me—I know my wife,' he replied smoothly. She was a woman who still had not learnt her lesson about meddling in his affairs. A woman who had gone behind his back *yet again* and betrayed his confidence.

Drakon snorted derisively, as if he was far from convinced by Theo's words, then held out his hand to shake on their deal.

'We're finished here,' he said. 'Don't let me keep you from your other business.'

Theo shook his hand firmly, a wry lift of his brow the only indication of what he thought about Drakon's clumsy dismissal.

He left the hospital and headed straight back to the hotel. He could not believe what had happened. He had finally acquired the island for his aunt—but all he could think about was how Kerry had betrayed him. Again.

Kerry looked down at Lucas, already sleeping soundly. She walked out of the nursery and closed the door quietly, biting her lip distractedly.

She'd been in a permanent state of agitation since Drakon had called her to the hospital the previous day. She'd been determined not to do or say anything that would displease Theo, but it hadn't made any difference—because Drakon already knew everything.

He'd told Kerry the story of Theo's aunt and uncle, and how they'd lost the island. And then he'd simply watched her response as he'd quizzed her about Theo's plans. When he'd suggested that Theo might be buying the island in order to give it back to his aunt, her reaction had confirmed his guess was correct.

She felt awful for inadvertently giving Drakon the verification he was looking for—but short of telling him an outright lie she hadn't been able to hide the truth.

Although she knew Theo would be furious with her, she had decided to tell him what had happened as soon as possible. But he never seemed to be around. She'd tried to call him, but he was always in meetings. And in any case it wasn't the kind of conversation she wanted to have over the telephone.

She walked out onto the roof garden, hoping to calm her nerves, but somehow the heavy fragrance of jasmine seemed too overpowering, and the trickle of the fountain didn't soothe her as usual.

Suddenly she realised that she was thinking about the last time she'd waited for Theo on the roof garden, knowing that she was about to confess something that would make him angry. That time she *had* made a terrible mistake—and Theo had reacted by kicking her out of his life. This time she had not done anything wrong except *not* tell Drakon a barefaced lie to protect Theo's privacy. But she knew he would still be angry.

She turned to go back inside, but at that moment Theo appeared in the doorway.

'I'm glad you're home,' she said right away, pleased at how steady she kept her voice, despite the unease that filled her. 'There's something I need to tell you—something that happened yesterday.'

'You went to see Drakon,' Theo said, pre-empting her confession.

Kerry looked up at his face and felt herself tremble. Whether he'd meant to or not, Drakon had put her in a terrible position. And now she had to try to explain it to Theo.

'He sent me a message,' Kerry said. 'I felt I had to go right away—he's been so unwell that I didn't think I should delay.'

'I've also been to see him. In fact I've just come from the hospital now,' Theo said, partially drawing a sheaf of papers out of his briefcase. 'The island is now mine.'

'Oh!' Kerry gasped, relief running through her as she watched Theo return the documents to the safety of his case. 'Oh, that's wonderful.'

Then she looked back at his face, and a bundle of

nerves tightened inside her as she realised her relief had been misplaced. Despite the fact he'd finally bought the island he was furious.

'Why aren't you pleased?' she asked. 'You've got what you wanted.'

'I wanted a wife who understood not to meddle in my affairs,' he grated.

'I didn't meddle!' she said incredulously, a spike of annoyance stabbing into her.

'You told Drakon things that I'd told you in confidence,' he said.

'No, I didn't!' Kerry exclaimed. 'Drakon already knew. He just wanted confirmation.'

'So you gave it to him,' Theo said stonily.

'No, it wasn't like that. He told me what he knew—which was everything,' Kerry insisted. 'I didn't say anything—but I couldn't deny what *he'd* said. Short of lying, there was nothing I could have done.'

'You went against my wishes,' Theo said. 'Even though I made myself absolutely clear to you.'

'Did you want me to lie to a sick old man—tell him he was wrong about something he already knew to be true?' Kerry demanded.

'Don't try to turn this around,' Theo grated. 'You're not the martyr here.'

'And neither are you!' Kerry threw back at him, suddenly furious with the way he was treating her. 'You're acting like I deliberately set out to defy you!' she cried. 'Nothing bad has happened. You should be pleased—you've finally bought the island you've wanted for years.'

'Drakon would have sold to me sooner or later. That is not the issue,' Theo said, stepping closer so that he was looming over her—a menacing physical presence. 'The point is I cannot have a wife that I don't trust.' He moved closer. 'And I don't trust you.'

Kerry did not miss the threat in Theo's words. But rather than make her nervous they sent a wave of anger rolling through her.

'This isn't about *trust*,' she accused him. 'This is about what kind of wife you want—someone who is quiet and biddable, someone who never expresses her own opinion.' She paused for breath, still glaring up at him. 'In fact you don't want a wife at all. You want another employee—someone who'll happily jump to do your bidding and never challenge you in any way!'

Theo was staring down at her, his dark eyes glinting dangerously. She could see a vein throbbing at his temple and a muscle pulsing in his jaw.

'Whatever accusations you make—whatever defence you plead,' he said coldly, 'understand that I will not tolerate your continued interference in my affairs—private or business.'

'Don't try to intimidate me,' Kerry said, placing her hands on her hips and standing her ground as he loomed over her. 'A lot has happened since the night you threw me out—I'm not the same timid girl I was then.'

'Really? Then why are we right back to square one—arguing about how you betrayed me?' Theo demanded savagely.

'I didn't betray you—that's just how you've chosen

to interpret what happened,' Kerry said. 'It's impossible for you to accept that anybody else can ever have a valid opinion or be well motivated.'

She turned to the side for a moment, dashing away the foolish tears that sprang into her eyes as she realised it didn't matter what she said—Theo had already judged her. Whatever she did, he always construed it harshly. She drew in a steadying breath, lifted her head and looked him straight in the eye once more.

'You are a control freak,' she said. 'Everything always has to be on your terms. No matter what, you're always convinced that you know best—that your way is the right way.'

Theo glared at her, his heart thumping angrily in his chest. How dared she make such an accusation?

'Demanding respect from the people around me and taking charge of my life does not make me a control freak,' he said angrily.

'Never accepting that anyone else can ever have a valid point of view, always insisting that everything happens in exactly the way you envision it—even when the outcome is the same—*that* makes you a control freak,' she said.

'However you try to turn this around—to point the blame at me—I will never tolerate your interference in my affairs,' Theo bit out.

'Don't you realise how hypocritical you are being?' Kerry asked, her voice rising with exasperation. 'By wanting to control everything all the time *you* are the one guilty of interfering with other people's lives. *You* told Corban to put Hallie in rehab. *You* bought the island for your aunt with the aim of totally changing her life. And *you* forced me to come to Greece to marry you.'

'I want what is best for my family,' Theo said. 'There is nothing wrong with that.'

He'd only ever tried to do the right thing—for Hallie, for his aunt. And most importantly for Lucas. He would *not* permit Kerry to twist his good intentions.

'It's the way you go about it—refusing to see anything from anyone else's perspective,' she said. 'You told me how you couldn't stand your father meddling in your life. But I think you've put so much energy into single-handedly taking control, that you can never accept anyone else might have something to contribute.'

'Don't compare me to my father,' Theo grated.

'Why not?' Kerry demanded recklessly. 'You behave in the same way—riding roughshod over other people's lives.'

'You don't know what you are talking about,' he said, his voice throbbing dangerously.

She stared up at his furious face, and suddenly all the anger drained out of her. She couldn't bear to continue arguing with him.

'I can't do this any more—it won't make any difference.' She felt her shoulders slump with defeat. 'I feel like I'm constantly walking on eggshells. However hard I try I can't help making you angry with me.'

'If you kept your nose out of my affairs we wouldn't have this problem,' Theo said.

She lifted her head and met his gaze straight on. She

loved him—but she didn't know how they could ever make their marriage work.

'I just can't talk to you. It's pointless,' she said, feeling her heart breaking all over again. 'You'll never really hear what I'm saying. Whatever I do you'll just interpret it negatively.'

She turned to leave—there was nothing else she could do.

'Don't walk away from me.' He spoke through gritted teeth. 'I'm not finished with you yet.'

She stopped and looked up at him, feeling a wave of despair rising up through her.

'I know,' she said, her voice breaking with emotion. 'You never will be. Because we have Lucas you'll never be finished with me.'

Theo stood rooted to the spot, staring down at her with hostile eyes. But as she turned to leave he didn't try to stop her.

Kerry hardly slept that night. It was a welcome relief when morning came and she heard Lucas stirring in the nursery. She slipped out of bed quietly, although she suspected Theo wasn't asleep either, and went through to get him up and dressed for the day.

After their argument she couldn't face seeing Theo. And apparently he felt the same way, because he began working in his study very soon afterwards. Although it was a large apartment, she started to feel claustrophobic. Simply knowing that Theo was behind the closed door of his study, a dangerously brooding presence like a volcano waiting to erupt, made her feel uneasy.

So as soon as it seemed a reasonable time she put Lucas in his pushchair and went out for a walk. After the air-conditioned hotel it felt very hot and heavy outside—even though it was barely eight o'clock in the morning. The weather had been unsettled for a few days, so she'd put the rain cover on Lucas's buggy—something that was rarely necessary in the Athens summer.

She set off away from the bustling business district of the city, towards the winding medieval alleyways around the Acropolis. But she'd forgotten that the tourist area was slower to wake up in the morning and found the streets disconcertingly deserted, apart from a few shopkeepers mopping the marble pavements outside their small stores.

Eventually she found an open café and sat down to give Lucas a drink. She ordered cappuccino and baklava for herself, hoping the combination of caffeine and sugar might give her a boost. The air was so muggy that her sleepless night was really catching up with her.

But as she sat there, looking distractedly at the reflections in the shiny wet marble in front of the trinket store across the alleyway, she felt increasingly weary. And all she could think about was how much she loved Theo— and how he would never, ever love her. He'd broken her heart into a million jagged fragments once more. And this time she didn't know how she'd ever find the strength to pick the pieces up.

* * *

Theo watched his Aunt Dacia's face as the helicopter approached the island. He'd met her properly for the first time in his life that morning, and he couldn't quite get over how like his mother she was. It wasn't really the way she looked—it was more to do with the way she moved, her gestures, and particularly the sound of her voice.

It was a strange feeling, finally bringing her back to the island where she'd grown up with his mother. He'd been amazed and pleased that she had agreed to come with him so readily. After the way she'd refused to have anything to do with him—even slamming the door in his face once or twice, before he'd given up on direct personal contact—he'd been prepared for a lengthy process of persuasion.

She didn't speak as they walked along the ridge from the helipad, but as he glanced sideways at her he could see her eyes were shining brightly, and he knew coming back to the island was an emotional experience for her.

'I can't believe I'm really here,' Dacia said eventually, as they followed Drakon's assistant into the house.

'Does it seem very different?' Theo asked, as he held the door for his aunt. A wry smile flashed across his face as he remembered Drakon's terse comment that he didn't need help because the door stayed open on its own.

A lot had happened since that evening when he'd first brought Kerry to the island. His well-ordered life had been completely turned upside down. He was here, properly meeting his aunt for the first time, and fulfilling his mother's dying wish that he find a way to help her. And back in Athens he had a wife and son.

An unpleasant ripple of emotion went through him

as he remembered the argument they'd had the previous evening. The look of desperation in her eyes when she'd said she knew he'd never be finished with her had cut him deeply—unexpectedly so. As had the way she'd curled away from him all night, on the very edge of their large bed.

'The outside hardly seems to have changed,' Dacia said. 'And even the inside seems the same, apart from the furniture.'

'There are some maintenance issues—mainly with the olive groves and the traditional press that was used to make the oil,' Theo said, pulling his thoughts back to the present. 'But I've already made contact with several experts we could employ to get things back on track— if that's what you decide to do with the place.'

'These are the paintings I was asked to point out to you,' Drakon's assistant said, leading them into the whitewashed corridor. 'Now, if you'll excuse me, I'll go and check on the refreshments.'

'Oh!' Dacia gave a little cry and lifted both hands up to her cheeks.

Theo could see how much she was trembling as she walked closer, to look at the paintings that had been done by her late husband—the love of her life. Her head was tipped to the side as she gazed at them, and suddenly he saw that tears were running down her face.

A strange lump tightened in his throat and he reached into his jacket pocket automatically for a clean handkerchief. He stepped nearer and offered it to her, and then, without thinking what he was doing—maybe because she was so like his mother—he put his arm around her thin shoulders and gave her a reassuring hug.

She jumped slightly, and turned to look up at him with startled eyes.

Theo cleared his throat gruffly and dropped his arm stiffly by his side.

'Please excuse me,' he said, stepping back awkwardly. 'That was too forward of me.'

'No. You must excuse *me*.' Dacia looked up at him with sparkling eyes, shaking her head from side to side. 'Thank you so much for doing this for me.'

'It's nothing.' Theo brushed her thanks aside.

'It is everything,' Dacia said with feeling. 'After the way I turned my back on you and refused all your offers of help I don't deserve this.'

'I am pleased to have found a way to put things right,' Theo said. 'It was because of my father that you lost so much.'

'Because of your *father*—not because of you,' Dacia said. 'But I was so foolish I turned my back on my sister and on her boys. And now you've grown up to be such a wonderful, handsome man—I'm sorry that I missed so much of your life. That I threw my sister's good intentions back in her face.'

Theo looked down at her, completely lost for words. He knew that Dacia and his mother had never been particularly close. They'd been very different people—Dacia had liked to lead a simple life, and his mother had relished the high-paced, fashion-orientated life that marriage to his father had brought her. But it was sad that they hadn't overcome their differences before his mother had died.

'I'm sorry that I never accepted all your offers of help,' she said. 'Especially the paintings I returned unopened—that was unforgivably small-minded of me after the trouble you must have gone through to get them. I was so determined not to accept anything from your family that I hurt myself—denied myself the chance to have something that would have brought me comfort.'

'What made you change your mind now?' Theo asked. 'I was absolutely delighted when you accepted my call and agreed to come out here with me. But I must admit I was a little surprised to find you so willing.'

'I'm sorry,' Dacia said again. 'I'm ashamed to say that if it hadn't been for the elderly man who used to own this island contacting me and asking me to visit him in hospital, the chances are I still wouldn't have come to my senses.'

'What happened?' Theo asked.

'I went to see Drakon Notara. He told me that you were trying to buy his island so that I would be able to return to my old home,' Dacia said. 'I was shocked, and I think I would have walked away—but he is such an engaging old fellow. Once he started talking I found I didn't want to leave any more.'

Theo looked at his aunt, feeling a touch of irritation towards Drakon. He'd been busy—he'd seen Kerry in the morning, then his aunt that afternoon, and then finally Theo on the following day.

'What did he tell you?' Theo asked, uncharacteristically uneasy about what Drakon might have told his aunt.

'More or less his whole life story, I think.' Dacia smiled. 'About his dear wife and their love of nature. About how his greatest concern was to preserve the island as it was. He couldn't bear the idea of modern development ruining it—and that was where his interest in me came in.'

She paused and smiled apologetically at Theo, as if to soften what she was about to say. 'He wanted my assurances that I would keep you in check—make sure you kept to your word and didn't start building hotels here.'

Theo raised his brows, startled to feel a burst of ironic humour rip through him. Drakon was such a character. The idea that his aunt, a woman Theo had never even met properly before, would be able to hold sway over him was absurd. He'd build a concrete jungle on the island if he wanted to—*no one* told Theo Diakos what to do.

But then he found himself feeling an unexpected amount of respect for Drakon. That cunning old man was no fool. In fact he had completely got Theo's measure. He knew he had bought the island to mend bridges with his aunt, and that he *would* listen to what she had to say.

'I won't build any hotels,' he said. 'But you will have to decide what you want to do with the island. There are plenty of possibilities—from restarting the olive oil production to running small painting retreats like you used to.' He paused, suddenly realising that suggesting something that would inevitably bring memories of her late husband might be too painful.

'You don't have to decide immediately,' he continued. 'Take as long as you need to think about it. And if you feel that the island is not the right home for you now—that's all right too. We can still find a way to preserve what Drakon has started here.'

Dacia smiled, and turned to look back at the paintings hanging on the whitewashed wall.

'I'd like to send you the other paintings now,' Theo said, thinking about how they had caught Kerry's eye and spiked her curiosity. It had taken him years to find and then acquire work by his uncle. Most of his paintings were in private collections, and it was very rare that they came onto the market.

'Thank you.' Dacia smiled up at him warmly. 'But, you know, after all this time I realise that what I would love is the chance to get to know the people I foolishly shut out of my life.'

'Of course,' Theo said. 'I know Corban would be delighted to introduce you to his family.'

'And I would love to meet your wife,' Dacia said. 'Drakon clearly thinks the world of her. I got the impression that she was instrumental in his decision to sell the island.'

'Yes, Drakon's always been very taken with Kerry. I believe she reminds him of his late wife, back when he first met her,' Theo replied without missing a beat—but inside he felt an unexpected jolt.

He'd always known that Kerry would play a part in

the old man's willingness to do business with him—which was why he'd followed Drakon's request and brought her out to the island to meet him. But suddenly he was thinking about what she'd said the night before—that he was a control freak. That he always judged her negatively, never believing her involvement could be well motivated.

'The refreshments are ready.' Drakon's assistant spoke politely, interrupting his thoughts.

'How lovely,' Dacia said. 'Thank you.'

Theo turned to escort his aunt out to the paved area overlooking the Adriatic. Despite everything he had said the night before, he did acknowledge that Dacia was here now, with the minimum of persuasion, because of Kerry and Drakon's involvement. And he knew that if he'd done things his own way it might have been a much longer, more painful process.

'I've kept on all of Drakon's staff,' Theo said. 'It should make the transition of ownership easier. But of course you will be free to make your own decisions about staffing in due course.'

'You've turned my world upside down,' Dacia said, reaching out and squeezing Theo's hand. 'You can't even begin to imagine what this means to me. Thank you—thank you so much for doing such a marvellous thing.'

Theo smiled. He was about to say that it was nothing when suddenly he realised that might diminish how much it meant to Dacia to return to her island home. 'I can't take all the credit,' he found himself saying.

'I can't wait to meet your wife,' Dacia said. 'She must be a wonderful person to have in your life.'

'She is.' Theo smiled at his aunt politely, thinking about Kerry again.

Back when they'd first been together, he'd used to think of her as the perfect antidote to his fast-paced, pressurised lifestyle. She had been exactly what he was looking for in a lover—calm, beautiful and receptive to his wishes. Like an oasis of serenity amidst the cut and thrust of his life.

But Kerry had changed. She'd once been his perfect lover—but she was very far from being his perfect wife. She'd gone against his wishes. And she'd stood up to him, calling him a control freak.

His life had been so well ordered and organised, with everything under his control and nothing unexpected. That was how he liked it.

Did that make him a control freak? Suddenly he wasn't sure.

All he knew was that Kerry and Lucas had exploded into his world and nothing was the same. Nothing was predictable.

He was used to demanding immediate obedience from everyone in his life—but Kerry wasn't an employee. She was his wife. Did he really want the kind of biddable, spineless creature she had described?

Ever since he'd found out about Lucas he'd only ever done what was best for his son—he hadn't thought about what might be best for Kerry or for himself.

He remembered the look in her eyes when she'd said

she knew he would never be finished with her. The thought of spending her future with him had obviously filled her with despair—and for some reason that made him feel cold inside.

CHAPTER TWELVE

THE sound of thunder rumbled through the city, and Kerry realised with a sinking feeling that a storm was coming. The air was heavy and humid, and it seemed to press down on her as she trudged along the pedestrianway beneath the Acropolis. She was tired and, despite the atmosphere between herself and Theo, she wanted to get Lucas back to the hotel as soon as possible. But what seemed like a reasonable walk on an ordinary day suddenly seemed like a marathon.

The first raindrops fell as she turned out of the small backstreets onto the busy main road that lead to Syntagma Square. She'd always thought of it as a horrible wide thoroughfare, with what seemed like all the traffic in Athens speeding along it—but it was the most direct route to the hotel, and the place where she thought she stood the best chance of flagging down a taxi.

Then suddenly, with a monstrously loud crack of thunder and a flash of lightning right above her, the skies opened and the rain poured down.

Lucas howled as she hauled his rain cover over him.

He was keeping dry—but he wasn't used to being enclosed by the plastic cover, or to the horrendous noise of the rain pelting down onto it. Kerry was drenched to the skin in a second, but she kept on pushing the buggy towards home.

The rain was so heavy that the huge towering columns of the Olympian Temple of Zeus were almost invisible, even though they were only across the road from her. And within minutes wide torrents of rainwater were surging along the gutters—turbid and brown from a whole summer's dirt being washed off the streets in one go.

Lucas was howling so loudly that she could hear him even over the sound of the storm. It was impossible to flag down a taxi because she was too scared to get the buggy close to the gushing deluge of run-off water along the roadside. So she bowed her head into the rain and kept pushing towards home.

Theo was already back at the hotel when the storm hit the city. It was just a summer thunderstorm—but when he discovered Kerry and Lucas were out in it he felt a sharp kick of concern. He paced up and down his study, looking out at the torrential rain, wondering where they were.

Suddenly the sound of his mobile phone made him jump—it was Kerry.

'Where are you?' he barked.

'The National Gardens… Lucas is upset… I broke the rain cover and he won't stay under it…' It was impossible to hear her clearly over the crackling connection and the sound of the storm, but he just about managed to make out the location she described. 'I can't get Lucas home. Please...will you help me?'

The sound of her distress raked across his consciousness, setting his heart thumping urgently. She must be in trouble to call *him*—as far as he could remember in all the time they had been together she had never once asked for his help.

He seized a giant golfing umbrella and bolted from his study. A car could pick them up at the entrance to the gardens and bring them back to the hotel—but he could get there quicker on foot. He didn't want to leave Kerry alone for a second longer than he had to.

The rain stung his face as he ran, carrying the umbrella unopened in his hand, dodging pedestrians and jumping the rivers of water sluicing along the gutters. It didn't take long to reach the National Gardens, and he sprinted along the deserted paths towards the place where she'd said she was waiting.

At last he saw her—crouched down by the pushchair in the pouring rain, attempting to keep the torn cover over the howling baby at the same time as trying to comfort him. Theo's heart was in his mouth and he felt a powerful rush of protectiveness.

She looked up as he approached, and the forlorn look on her face cut him to the quick. An overwhelming urge to reach out to her and haul her up into his arms seized him. He wanted to kiss away her misery and make her forget her worries. But then a cold wave of bitterness washed over him as he remembered *he* was the one making her miserable.

He stopped abruptly beside her and hesitated. Suddenly, for the first time in his life, he didn't know what to do.

'It's all right—Daddy's here,' Kerry said to Lucas. 'I can pick you up now. We can hide under the umbrella together.'

Her words galvanised Theo into action. He opened the umbrella and held it over all three of them, then he reached out with one strong arm, supporting them as she stood up.

Apparently being in his mother's arms was all that Lucas needed, because as soon as he was cradled against her shoulder he quietened down. Theo saw the tension across Kerry's shoulders visibly ease, then she lifted her face to him.

'I ripped the cover,' Kerry said, trying to look at Theo across the top of Lucas's black curls. Her long fringe was sopping wet and plastered over her eyes. 'I folded it back for a moment, to try and calm him down, but somehow it got caught and tore. I couldn't keep the rain off him and walk at the same time.'

She lifted a hand to push her hair back, expecting to see an expression of displeasure on Theo's face—annoyance that she hadn't taken better care of his son. But the look of concern she saw in his eyes made an unexpected ripple of emotion run through her. His gaze was fixed on *her*—not on Lucas. And she had the strangest feeling that he did care for her, maybe just a little.

'I'm sorry—I took a shortcut through the gardens,'

she rushed on, trying to ignore the foolish feeling. She knew what Theo thought of her, and it wouldn't do any good to let herself get carried away by pointless wishful thinking. 'It was a silly thing to do. I should have taken shelter in a shop or café, not kept on walking in the rain—but I just wanted to get home.'

'You couldn't have known the cover would break,' Theo said, lifting his hand and brushing a long wet lock of hair back from her face. His touch was gentle, and something about it made Kerry's heart skip a beat. 'You made a wise decision, putting it on the buggy today. I didn't even know there *was* a rain cover.'

Kerry gazed up at him, struggling to concentrate on what he was saying. The tender touch of his fingers and the concerned expression on his face were making her feel oddly light-headed.

It was completely unnerving. She *knew* what he thought of her—he'd made it painfully clear. But the way he was looking at her now made her long to give in to the fantasy that they could be happy together. That one day he might come to love her—the way she loved him.

Suddenly she felt her eyes burning with tears. She dropped her gaze, flustered by the unexpected surge of confusing emotions within her. She should not let herself pine for something that could never be. She was just setting herself up for a lifetime of disappointment and heartache.

'I'm sorry.' The words were jerked awkwardly from Theo's lips as he gazed into Kerry's misery-stricken face. The haunted look in her eyes reminded him agonisingly of the previous night—when staring into her future as his wife had filled her with despair. 'This isn't what you wanted.'

Suddenly he couldn't bear the thought that being with him was making her miserable—she deserved so much more.

He felt ashamed that he hadn't realised the truth sooner. It had taken his aunt's comment that Kerry must be a wonderful person to make him see what had been right in front of him all the time. She *was* wonderful.

She was gentle and compassionate, yet ready to stand up for what she believed to be right. She was overflowing with love for Lucas, and had showed unwavering loyalty to the people she cared about. She should not have to live her life in misery.

It was his fault she was unhappy. He'd brought her back to Greece in anger, expecting her to meekly do as she was told. He'd never given her any respect. He'd never considered the possibility that she meant well when she showed an interest in his life.

'It's stopped raining,' Kerry said, startling him out of his thoughts. She was looking at him with an expression of confusion. 'I'm sorry I called you—disturbed your work. If I'd lasted out a couple more minutes the storm would have been over.'

Theo looked around them in surprise and saw that she was right—the rain had stopped. A rich, earthy smell filled the air as the ground around them soaked up much needed water, and the heavy atmosphere that had pressed down on the city before the storm eased.

He folded the umbrella away and felt the sun on his face. But its warmth didn't reach through to his cold soul. *He* was the cause of Kerry's misery, and that thought cut him deeper than he would have expected.

'Don't apologise for calling me,' he said. 'I want you to feel you can always come to me—but I know I haven't done anything to make you feel that you can. After everything that has happened I can't blame you for not trusting me.'

Before this she'd never turned to him for help. And now he realised just how much that had hurt him. The fact that she had never contacted him about Lucas—had never wanted him to be in her life—had felt like a slap in the face. But he'd pushed it to the back of his mind, refusing to consider why it had wounded him.

'I do trust you,' Kerry said, looking at him earnestly. 'I'm ashamed that I didn't trust you enough to come to you the night Hallie crashed the car. I wasn't thinking straight. If I'd stopped for just one moment I would have realised I'd got it wrong.'

Theo stared down at her, suddenly realising the terrible truth. If she had come to him that night, the outcome for their relationship would have been the same. Even then, when their affair had been completely harmonious, he would not have been able to stand her challenging his actions.

'You were right when you called me a control freak,' he said unevenly, raking his fingers through his own wet hair. 'I didn't know. I take my need to be in charge of my life, of my business, too far—and I can never forgive myself for hurting you.'

As soon as the words were out of his mouth he knew it was true. But, even more importantly, another realisation was forming. It was as if the storm clouds in his head were clearing—leaving the truth standing bold and undaunted in his mind.

'I love you,' he said, his voice full of confidence and amazement at the same time.

Kerry stared at him in shock.

The thread of his conversation had already been disconcerting. She'd never expected to hear Theo admit that he had been controlling. And now to hear him tell her that he loved her was just too much to take in.

'I'm sorry,' Theo said, lifting his hand and cupping her cheek gently. 'I shouldn't have just come out with that—it wasn't fair of me.'

Kerry frowned, gazing at him in confusion. He was being kind to her. He'd said he loved her. But after everything that had happened between them—after their argument the night before—how could he be telling the truth? And why had he just apologised for saying he loved her? Nothing made sense.

'When I first met you I was drawn to your beauty,' Theo said, slipping his fingers beneath her wet hair to caress the nape of her neck. 'Then I discovered what a gentle, sweet-natured person you are. I think I started to fall in love with the woman I believed you to be— but I wasn't prepared for what happened next.'

'I let you down.' The words caught in Kerry's throat

as she thought about the terrible thing she had done. It wasn't surprising Theo had realised the mistake he'd made in sharing his life with her.

'No—I let *you* down.' Theo's voice was deep and resonant, and Kerry stared at his handsome face, transfixed. 'I wasn't prepared to realise that you were not just the beautiful, angelic creature I imagined you to be.' He paused. 'You are so much more than that—more than I ever deserved.'

'I…I don't understand,' Kerry stammered, finding it impossible to make sense of what he was saying.

'I controlled everything and everyone that came into my orbit,' Theo said. 'That was how I liked it—or so I thought—but I was so focussed on taking command that I never realised I was standing still.'

He drew her close and locked his eyes with hers, so that she could see the naked truth illuminated in their depths.

'But then you and Lucas exploded into my life—setting my cold, unchanging world in motion,' he said. 'I never knew what I'd been missing until I realised what you'd given me.'

Kerry stared at him, feeling her heart start to patter inside her. A warm feeling was spreading slowly through her body—but still she hardly dared to hope. What he was saying seemed too incredible to be true.

'I love you, Kerry,' Theo said.

Suddenly the pure, simple truth of his words wrapped around Kerry's heart like a tender embrace. She knew he meant what he said—and at that moment all her doubts disappeared.

'I love you too,' she said, her voice quavering with intense feeling.

She saw a flash of emotion pass across his face, but then he frowned, shaking his head in denial.

'How can you, after the way I've treated you?' Theo said. 'I've made you so unhappy.'

'It was partly my fault,' Kerry said. 'I was wrong not to tell you about Lucas. I should never have kept him a secret from you for so long.'

'But I'd thrown you out,' Theo said. 'It's no wonder you didn't contact me. I'd never done anything to make you feel it was safe to confide in me, or to ask me for help.'

Kerry hesitated, suddenly feeling unsure of herself. Growing up unwanted in her grandmother's house, she'd learnt not to ask for anything, never to expect too much. It had been the best defence against inevitable disappointment. But Theo wasn't like her grandmother. He'd been generous from the day she'd met him—and he'd never given her reason to doubt his willingness to help.

'I should have had more faith in you—and in myself,' Kerry said. 'Right from the start I never wanted to make myself vulnerable by asking for anything—but now I realise I was shutting you out.'

'Knowing you didn't want me hurt my pride,' Theo admitted, a wry smile playing on his lips.

'But I did want you—I always wanted you,' Kerry said. 'I was afraid of you rejecting me.'

She gazed into his eyes, feeling the love inside her growing, knowing it was real. This magical moment with Theo was real.

'I love you,' she said. 'I've always loved you.'

Suddenly his lips found hers, and he kissed her in the gentlest, most tender way she could imagine. She felt her happiness growing alongside the blossoming love she felt for him.

'We've wasted so much time,' Theo said, drawing back and looking down at her, his eyes burning with emotion.

'We've been on a journey,' Kerry replied, thinking how much they'd both learnt on the way. How much they'd both grown. 'But now we're finally together.'

'You are the centre of my universe,' Theo said. 'Without you my world stops turning. Please believe that I'm never going to let you go again.'

Kerry smiled and eased the sleeping baby away from her shoulder before placing him gently in the pushchair.

'I'm not going anywhere,' she said, reaching up and drawing Theo towards her with newfound boldness. 'But first, please take me home—and get me out of these wet clothes.'

0509_SC_01/06

★ *More passion,*
more seduction,
more often... ★

**Modern™ and Modern Heat™
available twice a month
from August 2009!**

◉ 6 glamorous new books
1st Friday of every month

◉ 6 more glamorous new books
3rd Friday of every month

Still with your favourite
authors and the same ★
great stories!

Find all the details at:

www.millsandboon.co.uk/makeover

★

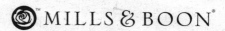 MILLS & BOON®

★

MILLS & BOON

MODERN

On sale 3rd July 2009

THE GREEK TYCOON'S BLACKMAILED MISTRESS
by Lynne Graham

Dark and utterly powerful, Aristandros Xenakis wants revenge –
to see her niece, naïve Ella must become his mistress!

RUTHLESS BILLIONAIRE, FORBIDDEN BABY
by Emma Darcy

Notorious Fletcher Stanton is determined never to take a
wife – but now his inexperienced mistress Tamalyn is
pregnant with his forbidden baby...

CONSTANTINE'S DEFIANT MISTRESS
by Sharon Kendrick

Greek billionaire Constantine Karantinos wants his heir. He
summons Laura to Greece, but his child's mother is less dowdy
and more wilful than he remembers...

THE SHEIKH'S LOVE-CHILD
by Kate Hewitt

When Lucy arrives in the desert kingdom of Biryal, Sheikh
Khaled has changed into a harder, darker man than before. But
they're inextricably bound – he is the father of her son!

THE BOSS'S INEXPERIENCED SECRETARY
by Helen Brooks

For the first time, awkward Kim feels desired! But she must
resist, for her powerful playboy boss Blaise will never offer
her anything more than a temporary affair...

Available at WHSmith, Tesco, ASDA, and all good bookshops
www.millsandboon.co.uk

0609/01b

MILLS&BOON
MODERN™
On sale 3rd July 2009

RUTHLESSLY BEDDED, FORCIBLY WEDDED
by Abby Green
Ruthless millionaire Vincenzo seduced Ellie and cruelly
discarded her. But she's now pregnant! The Italian will claim
her again…as his bride!

THE DESERT KING'S BEJEWELLED BRIDE
by Sabrina Philips
Kaliq Al-Zahir A'zam was outraged when Tamara Weston
rejected his marriage proposal. Now Tamara will model his royal
jewels – and deliver to him the wedding night he was denied…

BOUGHT: FOR HIS CONVENIENCE OR PLEASURE?
by Maggie Cox
Needing a mother for his orphaned nephew, magnate Nikolai
tracks Ellie down to make her his unwillingly wedded wife!

THE PLAYBOY OF PENGARROTH HALL
by Susanne James
Fleur would never make a one-night mistress – but she could
be the mistress of Pengarroth Hall – if only Sebastian
can overcome his allergy to marriage…

THE SANTORINI MARRIAGE BARGAIN
by Margaret Mayo
Zarek Diakos has decided Rhianne's wasted as his secretary.
He's in need of a bride: under the warm Santorini sun he'll
show Rhianne it's a position she can't refuse!

Available at WHSmith, Tesco, ASDA, and all good bookshops
www.millsandboon.co.uk

B/M&B/RTL

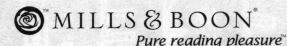

™MILLS & BOON®

Pure reading pleasure™

www.millsandboon.co.uk

◉ All the latest titles

◉ Free online reads

◉ Irresistible special offers

And there's more...

◉ Missed a book? Buy from our huge
discounted backlist

◉ Sign up to our FREE monthly
eNewsletter

◉ eBooks available now

◉ More about your favourite authors

◉ Great competitions

Make sure you visit today!

www.millsandboon.co.uk

2 Books
and a surprise gift!

We would like to take this opportunity to thank you for reading this Mills & Boon® book by offering you the chance to take TWO more specially selected titles from the Modern™ series absolutely FREE! We're also making this offer to introduce you to the benefits of the Mills & Boon® Book Club™—

- ★ **FREE home delivery**
- ★ **FREE gifts and competitions**
- ★ **FREE monthly Newsletter**
- ★ **Exclusive Mills & Boon Book Club offers**
- ★ **Books available before they're in the shops**

Accepting these FREE books and gift places you under no obligation to buy, you may cancel at any time, even after receiving your free shipment. Simply complete your details below and return the entire page to the address below. You don't even need a stamp!

YES! Please send me 2 free Modern books and a surprise gift. I understand that unless you hear from me, I will receive 4 superb new titles every month for just £3.19 each, postage and packing free. I am under no obligation to purchase any books and may cancel my subscription at any time. The free books and gift will be mine to keep in any case.

P9ZEF

Ms/Mrs/Miss/Mr ....Initials ....

Surname .... **BLOCK CAPITALS PLEASE**

Address ....

....

....Postcode ....

Send this whole page to:
UK: FREEPOST CN81, Croydon, CR9 3WZ

Offer valid in UK only and is not available to current Mills & Boon Book Club subscribers to this series. Overseas and Eire please write for details. We reserve the right to refuse an application and applicants must be aged 18 years or over. Only one application per household. Terms and prices subject to change without notice. Offer expires 31st August 2009. As a result of this application. you may receive offers from Harlequin Mills & Boon and other carefully selected companies. If you would prefer not to share in this opportunity please write to The Data Manager. PO Box 676. Richmond. TW9 1WU.

Mills & Boon® is a registered trademark owned by Harlequin Mills & Boon Limited.
Modern™ is being used as a trademark. The Mills & Boon® Book Club™ is being used as a trademark.